The
Menace
Within

ALSO BY URSULA CURTISS

The Menace Within

Ursula Curtiss

A Novel of Suspense

DODD, MEAD & COMPANY   New York

1 2 3 4 5 6 7 8 9 10

Library of Congress Cataloging in Publication Data

Curtiss, Ursula Reilly.
 The menace within.

 I. Title.
PZ3.C94875Me [PS3503.U915] 813'.5'4 78–13361
ISBN 0–396–07620–3

For my sister, Mary McMullen

Chapter 1

No doubt because of her function here, the nurse on duty at the intensive-care unit desk had somewhat the appearance of a bulldog adorned with lipstick and glasses. "Are you a relative?"

Amanda Morley had often wondered about the real usefulness of such a question, but in this atmosphere she only said obediently, "Yes. I'm Mrs. Balsam's niece."

The nurse made a decisive tick on a list in front of her, presumably so as to exclude any other would-be visitors, and tipped her white-capped head indicatively. "Room six twelve, at the end of the corridor."

Apart from a policeman sitting on a straight chair outside a closed door midway along, there was none of the emergency atmosphere—doctors clustered in consultation, plasma-laden trolleys being pushed at speed —that Amanda had somehow expected in this part of the hospital, with the busy brilliance of the intensive-

1

care unit behind her. Still, she tiptoed on the glossy black-and-white tile, gazing steadfastly ahead of her because somewhere nearby, surely visible if she looked, someone was crying quietly.

Mixed with her own anxiety was a cowardly streak of dread, even though the doctor had warned her. She arranged her face consciously, trying for an expression of fond but brisk concern—nothing to be really alarmed about here—and tapped lightly on the partially open door of 612 and went in.

It was a small room, scarcely more than a generous cubicle, filled with an indefinable aura which, if liquefied and bottled, would be labeled "Crisis." Amanda didn't know what measures had been taken nearly three hours earlier, when her aunt had been rushed here by ambulance; now, there was some kind of sinister apparatus under the bed and, at its head, a stand holding intravenous solution. The nurse who was checking its control, blocking the patient from view, turned at Amanda's entrance.

"Hi," she said brightly and at normal pitch. "Isn't it cold out? And that *wind*. I was just telling Mrs. Balsam she isn't missing a thing in the way of weather."

She was young, but obviously knew what she was about; without winking or grimacing she had struck the note. She turned back to the bed. "Comfortable now? I'll leave you alone with your company for a little while, okay?"

Rhetorical questions, because since her sudden stroke Jane Balsam had been unable to speak.

The nurse departed. Amanda walked the few steps to the bed, bent and kissed her aunt's cheek, said as she unbuttoned her coat, "Well, this is a pretty kettle of fish."

It was a talisman kind of phrase—as a family, the

2

Morleys had tended to avert tears by a near levity which frequently shocked other people—and the unparalyzed left corner of Mrs. Balsam's mouth tried to acknowledge it. Her eyes could not.

Amanda sat down and began to talk matter-of-factly. She would have been here earlier if she'd known, but of course Dr. Simms didn't have her office number and hadn't been able to reach her until she got home. "So I didn't stop to pick up nightgowns and cologne and things. I'll bring those in the morning."

The doctor had prepared her for the stony down-pulling of the right side of her aunt's face, and even the look of intense fear. "She's very frightened about her condition, and with good reason, I'm afraid. She's sixty-seven, and I've been after her about her blood pressure for years. Of course, twelve hours or twenty-four may give us an entirely different picture. Reassure her, if you can. That'll do more than anything else at this stage."

Reassure her—struck down, unable to communicate: the vocal and witty aunt, her father's eldest sister, with whom she had spent her final growing-up years after her own parents had been killed in a sailing accident on a vacation with friends in California. Gerald Balsam had been alive then; he had been dead for a year now.

It was astonishingly hard to maintain what was, in effect, a monologue; reflective little silences were comfortable only when the other person could break them at will. The December wind, icily cold as the nurse had said, pressed against the window in its stingy folds of institutional beige. Even with her coat off Amanda was uncomfortably warm. It crossed her mind that many people discharged from overheated hospitals in winter must fall instantly prey to pneumonia.

But that would scarcely do as a topic of conversation.

3

"Don't worry about your plants," said Amanda. Mrs. Balsam had a whole roomful of them in her recently acquired house, in pots and planters and on stands and benches, and had plans of converting this area to purposes of solar heat. "I may not have quite your thumb, but I'll water them."

The spiky-lashed, hazel-green gaze, very like Amanda's own, burned back at her.

I'm missing something here, thought Amanda, and remembered. "Oh, and don't worry about Apple either. I'll feed her and tuck her in for the night. Or I might take her home with me, just for a day or two, until we hear what the doctor says. I'll feed and water Drougette too, so don't concern yourself about that."

Apple, more formally Dreamspinner's Golden Apple, was Mrs. Balsam's cherished young Afghan hound, Drougette a palomino mare she was boarding for friends. The horse had escaped from its somewhat inadequate corral two nights earlier, causing Mrs. Balsam to roam the area for an hour before she caught it, and the dog was an occasional roamer, like most of her breed, so why, in answer to the assurance of their being taken care of, was a tear forming and then falling on Mrs. Balsam's cheek—not felt, not brushed away?

Because up until early that afternoon she had been a well and active woman, able to perform these chores herself, as well as a pretty one?

"Aunt Jane," began Amanda helplessly, "don't—"

Don't what? Be terrified because she had had a stroke massive enough to paralyze her right side and deprive her of speech? Amanda was saved from any such ludicrous injunction by the entrance of the nurse, who took a glance at her patient and said at once, "I think Mrs. Balsam would like to rest now."

Amanda stood, buttoning her coat, ashamed that she

was grateful. She said to the marred and flaring-eyed face on the pillow, "I'll be back in the morning, with whatever you were reading as well as some other creature comforts," because in spite of the hooding of the right eye her aunt's alertness did not seem to be at all impaired.

There was a sudden small thrash from the bed. "There, now, we're responding," said the nurse, but the flip of her hand was dismissive, and Amanda left.

Outside it was bitter indeed, with a wind that wrenched threateningly at the car door when she reached it, running, head down. As she had promised, Amanda set out for the house near the mesa twelve miles away.

Strings of colored lights and tinsel dipped and swung over the streets, clogged with desperate, last-minute shopping traffic. As the city fell behind, Christmas trees on lawns or behind picture windows took over, and then Amanda was in luminaria territory: the lighted long-burning candles in brown paper bags partly filled with sand, tops neatly folded down, to guide the Christ Child. They made golden punctuations in the night by the thousands, outlining driveways and adobe walls and rooftops. Amanda had her own luminarias in place, but, a stern traditionalist in such matters, would not light them until tomorrow night, Christmas Eve.

Which brought to mind the already-wrapped white coral earrings and vivid silk scarf which could almost literally be pulled through a ring. How long—Amanda could not phrase it to herself in any other way—before her aunt would wear either?

There was no point in speculating upon how long she had lain immobilized a few yards from her front door, or the horrifying fact that except for the arrival of a

5

United Parcel Service truck at about three o'clock she might still be lying there in the freezing dark. There were no immediate neighbors, and her car had shielded her from the view of what little traffic there was on the narrow climbing road.

It was not one of the two afternoons a week she did volunteer work at the very hospital she was now in, but she had obviously been starting off on an errand when something had prompted her to get out of the car, leaving the key in the ignition, the driver's door open, her handbag on the passenger seat. The stroke had felled her halfway along the flagstone walk.

The girl driver of the truck, arriving on the scene, hadn't wasted any time looking for the keys which turned out to be under Mrs. Balsam's prone form, but sped off to the nearest house to call the emergency number. A police car had responded along with the ambulance, and Amanda hoped sincerely that they had made a routine check of all the doors and windows. This was a lonely spot, and the house was going to be a concentration of blackness.

A rabbit leaped out of her headlights as she turned into the drive and parked behind her aunt's car. Before leaving the hospital she had accepted and signed a receipt for Mrs. Balsam's navy calf handbag—they were understandably not anxious to be in charge of cash or credit cards or other valuables—to which someone had restored the house keys, and as she approached the front door, leather case in hand, she listened for the Afghan's surprisingly baritone bark. Apple was a shy dog, but as long as she remained invisible she might have been a ravening mastiff.

Silence, except for the wind.

Apple had been in the car, then, grown impatient when her mistress did not return to it, bounded out, perhaps nosed affectionately around the stricken woman under the delusion that this was a game of some kind, gotten bored with it, and wandered off. She had probably been back a number of times since, crying plaintively to be let in for her dinner.

Amanda lit three matches with great difficulty before she was able to unite key with lock. Hand on the knob, she turned and called, "Apple?" but not very loudly, because she was curiously reluctant to pinpoint herself in this empty, windrushing dark, and opened the door.

The interior was even blacker than she had expected, as if walls and furniture, unaccustomedly left to themselves in the company of unlit lamps, spun out eager webs. Amanda had been in the house a number of times since Mrs. Balsam had acquired it four months ago, but it was still essentially strange territory, and she had to fumble for a light switch. In the last second before she found it, she had a flash of pure fear—something connected with fires and cave mouths?—and then, in a click, the house was ordinary and warm.

A tiny hall was suggested by low iron railings with eucalyptus massed in a stone jar at one side. The living room of which it was a part had overstuffed chairs in blue and violet and cream chintz and a tailored dark blue couch, pleasingly at home with the gray-blue shag rug which had come with the house and stretched up over a step to the small dining area which gave onto a see-through kitchen. It had somewhat the serenity of water.

A miniature Christmas tree dressed in pink and rose and silver bulbs flashed from the top of a bookcase. There were gleams of brass at the fireplace in one wall —and, on the nearest of the small end tables, two letters stamped for mailing, the clear reason for her aunt's intended return. Amanda glanced at them automati-

7

cally. One was for the gas company, the other addressed to a nursery in Michigan.

She proceeded through the house, switching on an occasional light as she went, and everything was locked. The peal of the telephone was shocking for some reason, and she ran back to pick up the receiver on a man's voice, pleasant, low, instantly doubtful. "Mrs. Balsam?"

It wasn't a good idea to advertise a house empty for the foreseeable future. "Mrs. Balsam isn't here right now, but this is her niece. May I take a message?"

She had the odd and fleeting feeling that she had flabbergasted the man at the other end of the line before he said, "No, that's all right, I'll call again," and, without further ado, hung up.

Her aunt hadn't mentioned the neighbors, if in fact they could even be called that, so this would be a friend from the Heights, where she had lived previously or else—she was included in the current telephone directory—someone like the Police Athletic League. Except that the caller had been unmistakably surprised at an alien voice on this line.

Here, Amanda became simultaneously aware of two things: first, that she was almost wolfishly hungry, having lunched at her desk on an apple and a few slices of Cheddar cheese; second, that the shock of what had happened to her aunt had completely driven from her mind some plan or commitment for the evening. Whatever it was, it couldn't be helped. It was certainly, thought Amanda, having to push down the familiar ache, nothing to do with Justin.

(Who was fond of her Aunt Jane, and had a right to know that she was in the hospital in a precarious condition. Call him, with the full knowledge that this was a perfectly legitimate excuse for hearing his voice again? No, or not yet, anyway, because who might answer his telephone?)

8

Amanda went into the kitchen. Unlike many widows living alone, her aunt kept a well-supplied larder, but although even at a glance the refrigerator offered stuffed olives and guacamole salad invitingly sealed under clear wrap she settled for a few cheese crackers, made herself a drink, and then, bold with the lighted house at her back, opened the door and called Apple ringingly and whistled.

Icy air shot past her, carrying very distant canine sounds ranging from the deep utterance of a German shepherd to the sharp excited barking of a poodle. Had the Afghan, less than a year old and left to her own devices for so long, joined a pack?

Keep calling at intervals; once Apple was within earshot she would come romping home. Amanda knew that she could not simply finish her drink, turn out the lights, lock the door, and drive away. She could and would lie to her aunt in the morning, if necessary—"Apple misses you but she's putting up with me for the time being"—but if the dog were permanently lost or stolen or shot the truth would emerge eventually, and Amanda did not like to think about the consequences.

Moreover, she was herself devoted to the silky, light-boned, glowing-faced Apple, who was given to sulking when she was scolded and toppling promptly over on her side if told that she was a pretty girl. Apart from wandering off for a period of two days during the first week in the new house, she had never stayed away from home before, according to Mrs. Balsam, and certainly not on a winter night which would be even colder before it was over.

In terms of the dog, Amanda refused to think beyond tonight. The morning newspaper was loosely folded on the couch, and she picked it up idly. There were still no leads in the disappearance of Ellie Peale, a young clerk with a thin, appealing face who had been abducted at

9

knife point from a convenience store two nights ago. A woman was suing a local café because she had come across the tip of the chef's thumb in her omelet; Amanda hoped she collected a mint, but could not help admiring a cook stoical enough to continue with his labors.

The teachers were considering a strike. Two prisoners had escaped from the state penitentiary, but this happened with the regularity of schoolchildren going out to recess. Amanda turned the page, gazed at the woebegone face of an orphaned spider monkey in a Detroit zoo, remembered with a rush of guilt what she was supposed to be doing tonight.

It was seven-fifteen, but she could at least call. She jumped up distractedly and went to the phone.

Sixteen feet below her, in a steel-reinforced concrete room whose trapdoor was concealed by tranquil gray-blue shag rug, the man who had killed Ellie Peale was beginning to pace dangerously, and to rage at the pain in his hand.

Chapter 2

The MacWillies, building the house near the mesa almost twenty years earlier, had been remarkably quiet about the bomb shelter included in its plans.

This secrecy was prompted by the moral question that accompanied such a structure: Who would they let in, if the shelter should actually be called into use, and who exclude? How would it be possible to say, "Sorry, no more," in the face of frantic entreaties? Because word would certainly spread.

As such places went, it was commodious, with bunk beds for the MacWillies and their two teenaged children, toilet, sink, shelves for a projected three weeks of supplies, an air filter system, a hydraulic jack as a hedge against entombment, and enough floor space for exercises. It was reached by means of a fixed fourteen-foot steel ladder under the floor just beyond the entrance to the kitchen.

Earl MacWillie, a building contractor who had de-

11

signed the shelter and done much of the work himself, had amused himself by making its access as invisible as possible, countersinking the ring in the trapdoor and cutting a flap for it of wood veneer that matched the surrounding floor. This also served to placate his wife, who had a mortal fear of the ladder and liked to forget that it existed at all.

Both son and daughter married and departed, variously to Maryland and New Jersey. As a thirtieth anniversary present to themselves the MacWillies had the house carpeted in deep-piled gray-blue, and a week later, the other part of their celebration, boarded a plane to visit their second New Jersey grandchild. The plane ran out of runway. There were no survivors.

Their children assumed, erroneously, that the bomb shelter was a matter of record. The bank's appraiser, attention on square footage and depreciation, did not notice—even Mrs. MacWillie had not noticed—the L cut with a razor in the fleecy new carpeting outside the kitchen. It was not a traffic area; it was simply a small stub extending off the dining room.

For all MacWillie's building expertise, the law required a plumber where there were pipes. The plumber in question had long since moved to another part of the state, but his helper had not. His helper remembered the bomb shelter very well, and, even before it became a refuge for his hunted half brother, had been using it for purposes of his own.

There was little that was not grist to Harvey Sweet's mill. A born opportunist who stole as naturally as he breathed, he did a little of everything—roofing, electrical work, furnace repair, drug-running from Mexico—and at thirty-seven would no more have dreamed of taking an eight-to-five job than of taking Holy Orders.

Managing to parlay a piccolo confiscated from the high-school music room into a broken-down secondhand car at the age of fifteen had left its mark.

Nature had equipped him well for his type of life. His features were regular and handsome, his clear blue eyes looked disarmingly candid, his very white teeth flashed frequently in his short woolly brown beard. Even while sliding someone else's money into his back pocket, he had something of the air of a Robin Hood.

In July he had brought back from Mexico not marijuana but brown heroin, the security of which, until he could arrange to sell it without danger to himself, posed a problem. His own house wasn't safe for long. His wife worked; so did he, quite often; he had a number of friends who suspected his activities and to whom he owed money.

The bomb shelter on which he had worked years ago presented itself as the ideal cache, if only he could get into it—but the MacWillies had been killed in a plane crash and the house was on the market, with viewers coming and going unpredictably. To break in would only focus police attention on the place. Sweet waited, unable to dismiss the shelter from his mind, and one September day when he drove by the real estate sign was gone, there was a car in the drive and the living room draperies were open, a great fringey golden dog was bounding about on the sandy rise against which the house was built.

Further surveillance showed him that a white-haired old lady was the only occupant. The dog looked valuable. As a kind of throw-away gift Sweet was good with animals and he had no difficulty in kidnapping it, overcoming its timidity by throwing sticks for it well out of sight of the house and finally offering it a beef bone.

His wife, Teresa, strikingly pretty and startlingly ill-natured, said when he arrived with his cargo, "I'm not going to have that thing in here."

"Yes, you are." Sweet was pleasant, but this tone had more than once preceded the infliction of a black eye.

"Where did it come from?"

"I'm keeping it for a friend. Don't let it out, I'll take it for a walk later."

Sweet watched the newspapers, and was pleased but unsurprised when, two days later, a reward was offered for the return of "Golden Afghan female, purple suede collar, lost vicinity west mesa." He telephoned the number given, and, with the dog at the other end of a piece of clothesline, presented himself half an hour later at the door of the MacWillie house.

The woman who let him in, and introduced herself as Mrs. Balsam when she had extricated herself from the dog's standing, full-stretch caress, was as overjoyed as he had hoped. "I can't tell you how glad I am to have her back. I suppose I ought to pen her, but she does love to run so, don't you, bad Apple? Where on earth did you find her, Mr. —?"

"Sweet. Harvey Sweet. She was wandering around in a trailer court near my house late last night, and I could tell she was lost. I was about to call the animal shelter to see if anybody had been asking about her when I saw your ad. Oh," said Sweet, making dismissive motions as Mrs. Balsam began to address the point of a pen to a check, "I don't want any reward."

She turned surprised greenish eyes on him.

"I have a dog of my own, a setter," said Sweet simply and falsely.

He had intended to put her under obligation, and he succeeded. Mrs. Balsam tried to insist, and then said that he must at least let her pay for his gas, and—a fragrant aroma had begun to waft out of the kitchen— have a cup of coffee.

14

From the living room, Sweet studied her as she moved lightly about on sandalled feet. She was in her sixties, he guessed, but not the kind of sixties he was familiar with: either stringy or mountainous, with baby-sitting for grandchildren the social event of the week. She was tanned and slender, her hair more silver than white. Her left hand dazzled when she moved it. As if aware of his scrutiny, she paused fractionally when she had turned, holding a pair of flowered pottery mugs, and cast an inspecting glance into what was obviously a mirror in the inner wall.

It was nearly midmorning and there he sat, casual and unhurried in striped jersey and jeans. Mrs. Balsam asked with friendly curiosity what he did, and Sweet said, more accurately than she could guess, "Just about anything. As a matter of fact, I did some work on this house when it was built."

Here, because it was scarcely a standard feature, she would make some reference to the bomb shelter—but she only arched her eyebrows at him. "Really? That *is* a coincidence. It seems like a very solid house, although of course winter is yet to come."

Her brilliant gaze was absorbed and in-turned; Sweet could almost hear her trying to think of some work to give him by way of repayment. The dog, having finished the first wild rummaging in its dinner bowl, came and placed its long golden head on his knee, plainly regarding him as the agent of deliverance. Mrs. Balsam said suddenly, "I don't know whether you do this kind of thing, Mr. Sweet, but . . ."

She was, she said, going to board a mare for friends later on, but although horses had obviously been kept here at one time—there was a stable capable of holding two—the corral did not seem particularly secure to her. Perhaps he'd take a look at it.

She led the way along the hall to a door which

15

opened on a side patio. Sweet, instinctively cataloging his surroundings as he followed, threw an examining glance at the carpeting which covered the entrance to the shelter. How much of a problem to loosen it, peel it back, replace it—not once but a couple of times? It didn't really trouble him, now that he had actually gained access to the house.

The corral, partly shaded by a giant cottonwood tree, was very insecure indeed. Sweet pointed out a couple of rotting posts that would have to be replaced, and yanked at a strand of wire which broke in his hand. He agreed to shop around for materials and give Mrs. Balsam an estimate even though there was no hurry; the mare would not be arriving until the first of December.

The Afghan accompanied him dotingly to his truck. Sweet drove away, exhilarated, the first hurdle cleared. He had a strong suspicion that Mrs. Balsam had never so much as changed a faucet washer in her life and that before long he would be doing minor odd jobs. Inside the house.

When he returned home with the length of clothesline which Mrs. Balsam had meticulously handed back to him, Teresa was cleaning the kitchen with shattering force, furious because she was sure something was being kept from her. Like most people given to easy rages, she had an impetuous tongue.

"I hope you got paid something for keeping that animal and then driving all over creation with it."

"I did it as a favor," said Sweet, suddenly bemused. Was it possible that Mrs. Balsam did not even know about the steel-reinforced concrete room beneath her feet? No, that couldn't be.

Teresa refused to leave it alone. She flung around from the sink, tossing back her long black hair, placing her hands on her hips. "That dog wasn't something to do with Claude, was it?"

16

Claude, the much younger half brother of whom Sweet was fiercely protective, was at the center of most of their frequent quarrels. After their marriage Teresa had discarded all pretense of liking him, resented her husband's occasional financing of some small venture which always turned out to be useless, shuddered at Claude's looks, gone so far, on one disastrous evening, as to say, "If you ask me, there's something wrong with him."

From a physical point of view, it was difficult to believe that the two men had had the same mother. Whereas Sweet had an appearance of straightforwardness and quick intelligence, a hand seemed to have been passed lightly over Claude's features while they were still malleable, flattening the nose a little, drawing the dark eyes to a narrow unreadable length, creating wide sullen cheekbones. With his peculiar litheness, and the hair he wore at a shaggy length, it would not have been surprising to see him at the edge of a forest clearing, blowgun in hand.

Sweet, pleased with his own looks, had always felt troubled and obscurely guilty about Claude's, and championed and indulged his half brother as a result. He had occasional moments of uneasiness about the streak of unpredictability which was beginning to show itself at closer intervals—and would then attribute this disloyalty to Teresa's influence, and turn upon her the more furiously.

Now, however, he only said, "Are you out of your mind? Claude's scared to death of dogs," and drank a quick beer and drove into town to shop around for posts and wire. The next day, he started work on Mrs. Balsam's corral.

Contrary to his usual practice, Sweet did not cheat his new employer out of a penny, and it was only his habitual deviousness that made him fasten two strands of wire very lightly at one corner. He had no clear motive for this, any more than he had had for inserting an empty beer can into the heating duct he had installed in an eighty-thousand-dollar house a few months earlier; it was like a form of doodling.

Mrs. Balsam was pleased with his work and at the reasonable price he asked for it. On the point of paying him, she said, "Oh, just a minute. While you're here—"

The nights were turning chilly, and the wall heater in the living room had a pilot light which kept going out. While Sweet was testing it, the telephone rang. He listened alertly while he unscrewed a plate, emitting little whistles of total absorption in his job, and learned that, unlikely though it seemed, Mrs. Balsam worked two afternoons a week and was being asked to change her hours.

"Well, actually, Mrs. Williams, two to six on Fridays would be better for me, because the library's open late that night and I could stop by on my way home and have one less errand for the weekend. Do you still want me to do Tuesdays, or do I move up to Wednesday? . . . All right, let's stick with Tuesdays—" she sounded a little airy for an employee "—and I'll be there tomorrow."

Tomorrow was Friday. Sweet got up from his inspection of the wall heater and announced truthfully that it needed a new thermocouple. "Run you about twenty-three dollars."

A cloud moved briefly over the sun, shadowing the room with a suggestion of the darkness to come, and Mrs. Balsam asked anxiously, "Do you think you could do it today?"

Not even a close observer could have detected any

18

elation in Sweet's casual nod and glance at his watch. "I can go into town right now. I might have to try a couple of places, though. That heater's an old make."

"I'll be here," said Mrs. Balsam cheerfully. "Give a loud bang on the door when you come back, because I'm repotting some plants."

Sweet said that he would, and called as she disappeared down the hall to the plant room, "I'd better take this one with me."

He did take the malfunctioning thermocouple. After a swift and soundless exploration of the handbag on the floor beside the couch, he also took Mrs. Balsam's house keys.

The next afternoon, armed with a tack hammer and a flashlight, Sweet let himself in at the patio door, instinctively quiet although he knew from the absence of the car and the unchecked roaring of the Afghan that Mrs. Balsam was gone.

The dog was enormously glad to see him, and stood breathing fondly into his ear while he knelt on the carpeting where he remembered the trapdoor to be. He had begun loosening it before he discovered the razor cut in the fleece, invisible except to someone in this closely scrutinizing position. He got the heavy door up, aimed the flashlight beam into welling darkness to orient himself, and descended the steel ladder.

Above him, the Afghan cried plaintively at this loss of a playmate. Sweet located the light switch, snapped it on, and was almost twenty years back in time.

The shelter was surprisingly cold, and had the indefinable odor of all subterranean places. The mulberry-colored wool blankets were still on the bunk beds. The shelves were bare of canned goods, but a five-gallon bottle of distilled water remained.

Bags of a moisture-absorbing chemical hung at intervals from one of the steel beams in the ceiling, and Sweet reached up and hefted one speculatively. It weighed at least a pound, and would make an ideal repository for drugs or the other items which passed into his hands from time to time and could not be marketed right away: silver and turquoise jewelry, watches; once, the entire gold supply of a jewelry-making acquaintance who thought that people might be getting tired of silver and turquoise.

Still, for all its stamped-in familiarity—it was the first and last bomb shelter he had ever encountered—something about the place puzzled Sweet. There was an electric heater: When he switched it on its coils began to tick at once. He sent a roving glance along the bench for spreading the moisture absorber to dry periodically, and on the floor at one end was a manila folder.

It was labeled "Warranties" and held documents and service contracts for kitchen appliances. One of them, covering a dishwasher, was dated 1974, and that explained the small oddity. In spite of its chill and its cellar odor, the shelter had not had the air of a place abandoned for eighteen years or even ten, because MacWillie—until the ladder got to be too much for him?—had been storing records here.

The Afghan gave an imploring bark, and although it was clearly addressed to him alone Sweet snapped off the light and mounted the steel rungs as swiftly as if it had contained a warning. He let the trapdoor down, secured the few inches of carpet he had loosened, brushed the curling gray-blue nap concealingly into place with his fingers. It was with a real sense of shock that, straightening and turning, he came face to face with himself in a narrow oval mirror, so placed that it

20

reflected a strip of front lawn as well. Anyone approaching from the driveway—

Nobody was approaching; still, he let himself out the patio door with speed, having to thrust back in the eager face of the dog who had plainly thought they were going to spend the afternoon together.

He mused idly, as he drove home, about the extraordinary merits of the shelter, granted a homeowner of predictable habits. How likely was a woman of Mrs. Balsam's age to navigate that ladder often, if at all? If a man had to disappear for a day or two . . .

This was akin to premonition. It was only September, and Ellie Peale would not die for some time yet.

Chapter 3

"... so you can see how it went straight out of my head until this minute," said Amanda into the telephone when she had given a fast précis of events. "Were you able—you've found someone else, I hope?"

"No," said Maria Lopez.

It was possible to sound tight-lipped over a single syllable. Amanda saw, as on a television screen, the packed suitcases waiting beside her neighbors' front door; the two older children beginning to hop with impatience to the accompaniment of, "Will the airplane wait for us? Will it?"; the Lopezes glancing at their watches and going distractedly to a window to see if Amanda, who had volunteered to take their infant daughter over Christmas while they flew East for a family reunion, was home yet.

It had seemed so simple then. Rosie Lopez was a waiflike two-year-old just beginning to walk about on little bow legs, with big mournful dark eyes and, very occasionally, an abashed smile as worth watching for as the aurora borealis or the blooming of a rare orchid. She suffered from a disease which prevented her from gaining any nourishment except by way of massive vitamin doses, and the Lopez doctor had advised against a long plane trip for her. On the other hand, it was going to be the last Christmas for Maria's mother.

Amanda cleared her throat. She knew where her duty lay; it was just that, at the moment, it had a last-straw aspect. "Why don't you bundle Rosie up and bring her over? I have to wait for a dog, and if it gets very late we'll spend the night here."

In order to correct any impression of lunacy, she gave clear directions, and Maria said, "Oh, Amanda, I'll leave you all my money. We're on our way."

And what, wondered Amanda as she hung up, was she going to do with Rosie when she went to the hospital in the morning? Leave her in the sixth-floor waiting room with a toy of some kind under the eye of a friendly nurse. White uniforms were as familiar to her as her own diminutive clothes, and few people could withstand her.

Meanwhile, this interval had better be used for feeding the palamino mare. Somehow it had sounded easier in the warm and lighted hospital room. Amanda put on her coat, filled a pail with hot water in the hope of thawing the existing water in the barrel instead of uncoiling hoses, found a flashlight in a kitchen drawer, switched on the patio light, and went outside.

The corral was on the east side of the house, perhaps a hundred feet away. When she had gone half the distance Amanda turned the flashlight on, and at once caught a flash of iridescence as Drougette, standing patiently near the gate, swung her head around.

There looked to be enough water in the barrel to last

until morning with the addition of the pail's contents. Amanda found a stick, broke the ice, and poured, remarking, "I'd sip this if I were you, it has to do you all night," to keep herself company in her little ring of brightness surrounded by dark. Fortunately, as she had no idea where her aunt would keep wire cutters, there was a bale of alfalfa already open, and after a dubious appraisal of it—how much did Drougette eat at one meal?—she threw the whole thing into the corral. The mare addressed herself to it at once. Amanda put away a thought of having given her far too much, with resulting heaves or staggers or some other equine ailment, and stood for a moment in the friendly presence, listening to the night.

Had the dog pack, if the Afghan was actually with it, moved out of hearing range, or was it just that the wind had shifted? Neither; there was the full range of barks again, but certainly fainter. Amanda tried to strain Apple's baritone out of the rest, but it was useless at that distance. She called anyway, and by the time she got back to the house the telephone which had been allowed to ring twelve times had fallen silent.

Justin Howard replaced the receiver. Amanda had won their standoff, hands down, and he was both disappointed and annoyed that he couldn't tell her so. He supposed that she and Jane Balsam were doing some late Christmas shopping in concert, although Mrs. Lopez had mentioned other pressing arrangements and it wasn't like Amanda to forget a promise.

He was at a cocktail party, the kind where he wasn't sure what he was drinking except that it contained ice which kept bumping into his teeth. Could it be artificial ice? The hosts, whom he had never met before, were professional magicians, and the room into which he had excused himself to telephone was full of blow-ups of their act. A pair of unperturbed doves cooed and chortled in a cage, on the surface of which stood an upended black top hat with a lifelike white rabbit peering out of it. Around its neck was hung a hand-lettered card with enticingly tiny print: "For heaven's sake, where did *you* come from?"

Justin sieved another gloomy swallow out of his glass. (This was wine, or some illegitimate relative.) He tried Amanda's house again: nothing. He looked up and then dialed her neighbors; this time he would leave his name and a message, something he had been prevented from doing before by the frantic feminine spate bewildering his ear.

But the Lopez phone rang emptily too, as if it had joined the conspiracy. Justin took another swig of the innocuous liquid, and the door opened and the very pretty girl who had brought him here, the girl with whom he had thought he could forget all about Amanda Morley, came in and cried, "Justin, hurry up, that funny little man in the jeans and sneakers is going to stand on his head and do 'Casey at the Bat.'"

In plays, there always seemed to be French windows for such emergencies. There were none here, and Justin followed her.

Maria Lopez, who toiled intermittently in her vegetable garden and hung out great quantities of laundry every day, was almost unrecognizable in a suave cream pantsuit, blue eye makeup and a cloud of Chanel 19. In one hand she carried a small suitcase; cradled against the other shoulder was a mass of red-and-white plaid blanket, out of which Rosie's small face peeked before she buried it again.

Amanda, who knew this to be a shy expression of

pleasure, said, "I know you're in there, Rosie Lopez," and held out her arms, and the transfer was effected. Maria said rapidly, setting down the suitcase, "She's had her dinner, of course. I brought her pajamas and her vitamins and a few other things. We wouldn't do this to you, Amanda, what with your aunt and everything, but we'd never get seats tomorrow."

"Don't worry about it," said Amanda as a horn sounded outside.

"Oh, and a man called looking for you just before we left."

Amanda suffered a certain stricture of breath while looking casual. "Did he leave his name?"

"No. Well, I don't think I gave him a chance," said Maria, apologetic and edging toward the door at a second impatient blast of the horn. "I mean, I thought it was going to be you when the phone rang, and then when he asked if we knew where you were I went into this song and dance about having expected you back much earlier because of plane time and so on."

She tickled her daughter under the chin, adjured her to be good, and stretched up to give Amanda a quick cheek kiss. "I can't thank you enough. Merry Christmas and we'll see you soon. . . ."

Justin, thought Amanda when she had closed the door after her own injunction to have a nice trip; who else, when she had shut herself into a self-imposed nunnery for a month? She carried her blanket-wrapped burden to the couch, plopped it down, said to its owl-eyed inhabitant, "I'm going to put you to bed in a minute, Rosie, but first I have to make a telephone call."

She had last seen Justin at a post-Thanksgiving party at her house, which might be a lazy way to repay a number of obligations but was also a convenient one. She couldn't even remember who it was who had brought the Navy captain with whom she found herself closeted in a corner as the evening grew later.

She was astonished when she discovered that the hand she couldn't see was toying with her right earring, sending it gently swinging—and across the room, Justin, who must have been regarding her for some time, lifted his glass to her in a salute, put it down, and went quietly out.

Amanda caught up with him in her front hall, decorated mostly with an old-fashioned coat rack and a chest now piled with overflow garments. "Weren't you even going to say goodnight?"

"You were busy." Only to someone who knew the perfect civility of his usually mobile face was Justin very angry indeed, almost angry enough to wear an approximate topcoat home if he couldn't find his own in a hurry.

"Just because I spend fifteen minutes with a guest—"

"Fifty-five. Do you know what the trouble is, Amanda?" After some fairly ruthless treatment of overlapping sleeves, Justin had found his coat and was putting it on. "We've known each other too long, on and off. There are no more surprises—well, yes, there's one, thanks to your maidenly upbringing, but you've gotten bored."

He glanced past Amanda. "Here comes the fleet," he said, and grazed her temple with a kiss and departed without another word.

Later, attempting sleep first on one side and then the other, Amanda had to acknowledge that there was a tiny element of truth in Justin's accusation, except that it wasn't boredom; it was a sense of ease and comfort. She had been catching occasional glimpses of him for a couple of years—he was the nephew of a friend of Mrs. Balsam's—but although it was only within the last few weeks that they had actually discovered each other as independent entities, the groundwork of trust was there. Still, how would she have felt if Justin had spent an hour tête-à-tête with the female equivalent of a Navy captain?

She was not a teenager, to congratulate herself upon having provoked jealousy, and it was a question of manners as well. She tried to reach Justin the next day, without success, and like most frustrated apologies this one withered and died and was replaced with a little defensive anger of her own. He could have joined them in the corner, after all; he had a formidable presence when he chose, and there would have been no earring-twiddling going on under his stare. Moreover, he had dropped his bomb at a point where she had to go back and be hostess to six remaining guests.

But now, thought Amanda dialing, they could start all over again. She would ask lightly, "Were you looking for me, by any chance?" and then she would tell him about her aunt. No, she wouldn't tell him anything. He wasn't home.

Amanda put the receiver back. Her mind must have included the strong probability of Justin's getting into his car at once and coming here, because she felt suddenly very flat—but there on the couch was Rosie, torn between sleep and a grave astonishment at these strange surroundings. She did not demur at all about being scooped up for bed, only asking in a breathy whisper against Amanda's neck if she could have a banana, accepting a tangerine instead, and eating it with drowsy relish while, in the guest room, Amanda undressed her and put on the pajamas from the suitcase.

It was a pretty room, with white-painted furniture and chintz in marigold colors at the low-set windows. Rosie, whose crib was in much smaller quarters shared

29

with her older sister, was bemused, and pointed at the other twin bed and gazed questioningly at Amanda.

Would she sleep there? Yes, if the Afghan hadn't returned in an hour or so; with the door open she would be able to hear the scratchings, plaintive cries, and finally the stentorian barks with which the dog announced herself. Meanwhile, Rosie had gotten tangerine juice everywhere, including a little in her hair, and Amanda took her into the bathroom.

This was her aunt's; the guest bath was across the hall and off the plant room, which had been chosen for that purpose because of its exposure. The basin was occupied by a tube of toothpaste. Amanda opened the cabinet above to replace it, and stared.

Did a stroke sometimes have a precursor? Yes; she had read somewhere that people could suffer very small ones, causing subtle personality changes, without even being aware of the fact. Mrs. Balsam, a relatively lighthearted housekeeper when her husband was alive, had turned into something of a martinet after his death —"Like Englishmen in the jungle, I suppose," she had explained apologetically to Amanda—and she would never ordinarily have rummaged through her medicine cabinet this way, toppling bottles and vials and tubes.

Not that there was all that much there, because she was not a believer in panaceas for all occasions. Aspirin, the blood-pressure pills which she took only sporadically because they had side effects, deodorant, nonprescription eyedrops, sunscreen, rubbing alcohol, capsules for the hay fever to which Mrs. Balsam was prey, and something of which only a small red cap remained.

Amanda handed the damp washcloth to Rosie, said, "I'll be right back," and crossed the hall and snapped on the light in the other bath. This medicine cabinet contained far less, only the overnight amenities which a thoughtful hostess would provide, but the effect of a frantic, uncaring search was the same.

She felt a flash of compassion and guilt. When had she seen her aunt last? Two weeks tomorrow, when they had gone to see a group of touring aboriginal dancers, woolly-haired and ashy-gray, whose crouching prowl with knees lifted high, accompanied only by a strange clacking instrument and culminating in a leap, was enough to bring a chill to the spine.

Mrs. Balsam, coming back for a drink at Amanda's house afterwards, had seemed her usual self—"How would you like to have one of *those* running after you in a bad temper?"—but then Amanda herself had been somewhat preoccupied for a month. It occurred to her now that her aunt might have been taking a medication more dramatic than she cared to admit to, something in, say, the nitroglycerine class, and become panicky when she mislaid it.

In the other bathroom, Rosie was sitting on the floor and applying the washcloth industriously to her perfectly clean feet; was this out of deference to the guest room, or some association with hospital-bed baths? Amanda tucked her in, opened one window a cautious few inches, remembered her own spotlit feeling out in the dark with Drougette and drew the flowery curtains together. She was about to turn out the light when Rosie sat up in alarm and said, "Where my raggie?"

Luckily, Maria Lopez had remembered even in her haste to pack the strip of frayed and knotted cloth, no-colored from countless washings, which had once been the pink satin binding of a crib blanket and was now Rosie's cherished sleeping companion. Amanda put this dubious talisman into the small hand, said goodnight, and left the door half open so that light from the

31

hall streamed reassuringly over the foot of the bed. Then, although she was not fanatically tidy by nature, and certainly not in someone else's house, she straightened the contents of both medicine cabinets.

It was consciously the erasure of something warped, which she wished she hadn't seen at all.

The man in the shelter was ignorant of the jostling and toppling he had done in his one excursion out of hiding here. That had been obscured from him by his rage at the fact that he had found no antibiotic for his flaming, throbbing hand; no painkiller other than aspirin, to which he was dangerously allergic.

He had been driven precipitately below again, clutching a tube of antiseptic cream from which the cap had fallen loose, by the rumble of some heavy vehicle approaching the house. It wasn't an ordinary car, and it threw him into a frenzy of fear. Suppose the old woman had discovered somehow that he was here, suppose the dog had sniffed him out?

The cut, a deep jagged tear inflicted by barbed-wire two nights earlier, had infected at once. Climbing and then descending the ladder had been agony, and seemed to have extended the area of red around the puffed-out heel of his hand. If all went as planned he would be out of here tomorrow afternoon, but he couldn't bear this pounding, suppurating thing that long; he was beginning to have a terror of gangrene, of being shut up here with his own smell, of ultimately losing his hand.

The shelter was very cold. The electric heater had worked for only two or three hours, so he had spent most of his time stretched out in a lower bunk, blanket huddled around him. Now, by an association of ideas, it occurred to him that penicillin and other antibiotics

·were often kept in a refrigerator.

The old woman had to go to bed sometime. After his single expedition to the upper regions he thought he could find the refrigerator in the dark, and if in spite of all his caution she woke up and came out and found him, she was, after all, an old woman.

Chapter 4

There was nothing about her to suggest that by the middle of Christmas week Ellie Peale's name would feature in newspaper headlines, her face flash out of television screens. The pose used, a three-quarter view in which she gazed questioningly at the camera, seemed to indicate her own surprise at such a turn of events.

She was nineteen; small, five feet one inch, and slender, a hundred pounds, with brown eyes and darker brown hair. Her scrubbed appearance in the photograph was not the accident of being caught unprepared; she had a soap-and-water cleanness that was lively rather than prim, and a fastidious modeling to her mouth. She lived at home with her mother and stepfather, but like most of her contemporaries looked forward to an apartment of her own or at least a shared one. Hence her job at the Speedy-Q, a dim and not very successful little convenience store which sat by itself on

35

a country road, suffering from the lack of an adjacent gas station or hamburger place.

Harvey Sweet was surprised and mildly amused to discover, early in December, that his half brother seemed to be developing a crush on the girl. Although it was closer than the nearest shopping center, he and Teresa patronized the Speedy-Q only in cases of vital necessity because of the inflated prices, but he went in one evening for a dozen eggs and a better look at Ellie Peale.

His vague recollection was correct: She was nothing more than a high-school kid, who might have been passable given pompoms and a short cheerleader's skirt instead of her tailored beige shirt and brown slacks. He remarked jauntily as she rang up the price for the eggs that they weren't golden, just plain white, and was taken aback at the coolness of her glance above the distant little smile she gave him. She was suddenly not a yearbook stereotype but a girl who had been spoken to familiarly and didn't much care for it.

He advised Claude at the first opportunity that he was wasting his time. "I know that type. They're not pretty, so they make the first move and cut you dead."

He was aware as he spoke that it was that very remoteness and clear, dark-eyed pallor—the armor of a young girl working late and usually alone, although he did not recognize this—that was challenging to Claude. Still, Sweet reflected to himself after delivering his seasoned counsel, Ellie Peale was at least single; there was no husband to erupt with a shotgun.

There was a moral involved here as well. In spite of the frequent quarrels after which Teresa stormed back to her parents, or he hit her and walked off to spend morose, beer-drinking days with friends, Sweet was faithful to his vivid shrew, and disapproved strongly of any involvement with married women.

By the time Christmas week arrived, he had forgotten the whole thing.

There was always stepped-up activity for the police at this time of year: more parties and consequently more traffic accidents; shoplifters, the inevitable break-ins where householders had piled presents around a tree clearly visible through a front window, purse-snatchings and occasional assaults in the parking lots of shopping centers open late.

That was the expected. Early on Wednesday evening, however, came a report that two prisoners had escaped from the state penitentiary and were believed headed for Albuquerque. As one of them had relatives in the North Valley, local deputies assisted the state police in the setting up of roadblocks there. When an excited call came in from a man who had just witnessed the abduction of a girl clerk from a convenience store on Quivira Road, there was some delay in getting a car to the scene. (It did not facilitate matters that the caller had a slight speech impediment which, at this time of night, might have been interpreted as something quite different.)

By this time the manager had arrived for his routine closing-up, and was able to give the police Ellie Peale's name and address. The contents of the cash register were apparently intact—a distinct oddity, as scarcely a week went by without the holding-up of a convenience store somewhere in the city.

The witness, a dapper and entirely sober Mr. De La O, proved to be scarcely that at all. He had just pulled

37

up in front, he said, when the door opened and a black girl came running out and leaped into the passenger side of a car with its exhaust pipe sending out steady pulses of gray.

In the not unnatural belief that he was watching a getaway, De La O had kept repeating the car's license number aloud while he fumbled in his pockets for a pen and something to write on, with the result that when he glanced up, alerted by motion outside a van parked at the side of the store toward the back, and saw what had frightened the black girl, it was almost with the effect of an after-image.

There was only a bare light bulb at the corner of the building, and not a very powerful one at that, but another girl, this one in a light-colored shirt and dark slacks, was being forced into the van by a dark-haired man with a knife. Yes, he was sure she was struggling. By the time De La O had assimilated this astonishing fact, the van, gray or tan, he couldn't swear which, was speeding away, headed west. The light which should have illuminated its license plate was out.

He hadn't seen the man's face, but would describe his hair as medium length, his height as maybe five-ten or eleven. As to clothes, he could only say that they were darkish and could have been denims.

De La O, having already recounted his tale once before the arrival of the police, had now calmed down to a point where he was trying to buy a quart of acidophilus milk from the shocked and inattentive manager. The police took his name and address and agreement to sign a statement in the morning; then, accompanied by the manager, they tramped off to the back of the store to examine the exit. De La O took his milk and departed.

*　　*　　*

The name on the mailbox at the small house where Ellie Peale lived was Chenowyth. A Christmas tree glimmered in a picture window, a ribbon-tied wreath encircled the knocker. The carport, the deputies noted, was empty.

Mrs. Chenowyth, they discovered presently when she gave them a photograph of her daughter, had handed on her looks with an almost eerie faithfulness: Small, housecoated, she had the same dark eyes and pale slender face. She had been telephoned earlier by the manager, on the chance that De La O had seen another girl entirely and Ellie was at home wrapping Christmas presents, and had had time to assume a desperate calm. "I can't break down, I know. Ellie makes fun of me when I get—"

Her voice broke and then steadied. "What do you want to know? What can I tell you to help?"

It would be a good idea, said one of the deputies tactfully, if they could talk to her and her husband at the same time, to double-check little things and save everybody time and trouble.

"Roy. Yes, well, but he's at his company's Christmas party, and I don't know when he'll be back. You can't just walk out on parties like that, or they get—" Mrs. Chenowyth stopped, looking amazed at herself.

Then maybe she would call him there? They really thought she should.

They looked at each other when she had disappeared into another room, and shrugged. Most crimes of violence were family connected, and the man in question was a stepfather. The Christmas tree shone at them while they waited. A number of bulbs, larger than the others, had "Ellie" and a year iced on them in silver.

Mrs. Chenowyth came back. "One of the officers, a vice-president, had too much to drink, and Roy's driven him home. Please, let's get on with this, I can't bear—"

"What kind of car does your husband drive, ma'am?"

"A Volkswagen van," said Mrs. Chenowyth, still clearly too much in shock to consider the implications of this question. "Ellie had no boyfriends who would do a thing like this, I'm sure of that. She was dating a very nice boy in the summer, but he's gone into the army, in fact he's in Korea. Since then she hasn't really—"

"Color?"

"White," said Mrs. Chenowyth with some indignation, and then, told that they were referring to the van, "Brown. Tan, rather." Her eyes snapped wide open. "My God. You're actually sitting there and thinking—"

The front door opened and Roy Chenowyth came in, a monumental ash-blond man well over six feet and topping two hundred pounds, and to all intents and purposes that was that.

Santa Fe had responded with the name and address of the car owner whose license number De La O had so assiduously written down while missing almost everything else, and the deputies proceeded there.

It was a battered, thick-walled old adobe structure converted to apartments, built around a center courtyard with a statue of Saint Francis and a leafless mulberry tree now twinkling with strings of tiny green and white lights. The tenants were evidently a lively lot: At close to midnight music came from a number of directions, along with an occasional flurry of stamping that sounded like flamenco.

James Jepp, a short columnar man in rubber sandals and a karate robe which looked businesslike, ushered them into a huge firelit room obviously, from its pair of daybeds and kitchen fenced off by a counter with bar stools, the whole apartment except for a closed door which must indicate the bathroom. After the tidily matched furniture and blameless carpeting of the house they had just left, the decor here—bare polished wood floor, tables which were really sawn-off logs, a vivid, fraying wall hanging, candlesticks in frivolous places, and a single lumpy armchair—struck both deputies as Early Flea Market.

Jepp's companion, Beryl Green—she produced an ID card instantly and in silence, as if it were required of her often—was piquant-featured under her enormous Afro. She was also hostile and defensive; somewhere along the line she had learned to fear and distrust the police.

She said that she hadn't gotten a very good look at the man in the Speedy-Q when she went in to buy cigarettes because he and the clerk were at the dimly lit back of the store, sort of wrestling with each other. "I thought they were just, you know, fooling around." Then the girl saw her and screamed and the man turned his head.

"I got the hell out of there," said Beryl Green succinctly, gaze daring either deputy to challenge her. "You go mixing in things like that, you wake up dead."

She couldn't say whether the man was Spanish or Anglo. She only knew that he had dark hair and that he wasn't a kid; given a choice of ages she said maybe twenty-five. Pressed further, she said with a reminiscent shudder that he was funny-looking, and seemed to regret that at once, inspecting a thumbnail in adamant silence.

She didn't want to be involved; she might as well

have said it aloud. James Jepp, who had remained silent throughout, stirred and said in a surprisingly rich deep voice, "You told me he looked like he had a stocking mask on."

She turned her stiff frothy head and gave him a stare of strong resentment. "Did I? I don't remember."

A stocking mask flattened and distorted the features, and she agreed reluctantly and at last that she supposed this was what she had meant. As to the man's clothes, she could only suggest a Levi jacket or something like it. Would she be able to identify him? Furious look at Jepp—there was clearly trouble brewing in this alliance —she guessed she could try, and gave her telephone number at work in case it should be necessary to contact her there.

Belatedly, one of the deputies asked if she had seen a knife or other weapon. She said a firm no, but it wasn't an entirely trustworthy one under the circumstances.

Could De La O have imagined the knife, painting it in simply because there was a struggle going on between the man and the girl before she was forced into the van? As against that, he had been a capable observer in the matter of Jepp's license plate, and a responsible citizen, going into the empty store and using the telephone to call the police at once. And, outside, the girl had not repeated her scream. They would have to presume the knife.

A small and isolated business like the Speedy-Q would not have a humming trade trade during Christmas week. With the prospect of supermarkets closed for the holiday, people tended to do a comprehensive shopping when they bought their glacially frozen turkeys, so that late errands would be mainly to stores

42

which carried tree lights, bulbs, last-minute stocking presents.

Still, what kind of man would go boldly into a public place, without even an elementary disguise—Beryl Green was sure there had been no actual mask—and abduct a clerk? An estranged husband or a furiously jealous boyfriend—but, according to the evidence so far, neither existed in the case of Ellie Peale.

The effect suggested by a stocking mask, features blurred and slipped, was unpleasant from the outset, and the night was very cold. Where, among the luminarias and windows with silver-hung blue and red and green and gold, the illuminated rooftop sleighs, and the festive gatherings, was a small slender girl in only shirt and slacks? Where, having screamed and struggled, was Ellie Peale?

Teresa Sweet, returning home after delivering presents to her parents and sister and nieces and nephews, heard the telephone ringing as she let herself in, and then her husband's tense, "Christ!" and, "Where are you?" and, "Stay there," and something else, quietly into the mouthpiece, which she didn't catch.

She had brought back reciprocal presents, which she piled in a chair. "Who was that?"

"A friend of mine," said Sweet, brief and brilliant-eyed and quite safe in this economy; although Teresa was well aware of the source of their extra income, she did not care to know details. He was moving as he spoke, going into the kitchen for his jacket, coming back moments later to write on the message pad beside the telephone.

"Don't you get mixed up in it," said Teresa automatically, but Sweet only glanced at his watch. "Call that

43

number in . . . an hour and tell Mrs. Balsam that her mare is loose."

Balsam was an utterly strange name to Teresa. She began mystifiedly, "How do you know——?"

"An hour," said Sweet tersely, and was out the door. An exit from the next house coincided with his, carrying called goodnights and a fragment of choir song: ". . . all is calm, all is bright . . ."

Chapter 5

Amanda, with a vivid memory of the hospital room and the intravenous solution, felt callous as she took out the piece of round steak, the mushrooms, and the ripe tomato probably intended for her aunt's dinner tonight. But she was starving and deprived of her own kitchen, and even the best of refrigerators would not keep food indefinitely.

Here, a whole thicket of worries would spring up if she let it. But Mrs. Balsam was in good hands, the doctor had implied that only time would tell, and in the meantime the Lopezes' long-anticipated Christmas reunion had been retrieved. Amanda presently carried her plate into the living room and switched on the television set, low, so as not to wake the child in the guest room.

She had missed the first part of the local news, something to do with a downtown fire; there was a play of hoses and then the announcer appeared, promising to be right back. She always watched this man with great fascination because of his moustache, two thick, black downcurving wings which seemed to be attached directly to his prominent nose, creating for both a haunting impression of falsity. Occasionally, as if he had delved deeper into a disguise kit, he wore round steel-rimmed glasses.

When he returned, it was with the now-familiar inset of a young girl's face, turned and somewhat surprised, accompanied by a stark question mark. There was still no trace of Ellie Peale or the man described by two witnesses, and her parents had received no ransom demand or other communication. Anyone who had seen this girl, or the man who now appeared as sketched by a police artist, was to call the number flashed on the screen.

How casual, thought Amanda when the announcer had removed his preposterous nose and moustache into another period of invisibility: the takeover, and very possibly the taking, of someone's life on what had all the earmarks of a deadly impulse. Vans had grown in popularity over the last few years and there must be thousands of them in the city, with light colors predominating in a hot dry climate. The one which had been used to transport Ellie Peale could be standing quite openly in a driveway or parking lot.

A slice of bread danced its way across the screen, winking roguishly and piping that it was ready for anything—and, from outside and with no preliminaries, there was a deep commanding bark.

Amanda rushed to the front door, snapping on the outside light, and opened it. The Afghan stood there in the showering gold, silky hair blowing in the wind, ropy curlicued tail going still in puzzlement because this was not her owner.

46

"Come, Apple. *Good* girl," called Amanda wooingly, and Apple ducked her head in pleased recognition and took a prancing step forward and was cut off by the sudden emergence from nowhere of a tall, lean Doberman pinscher so black that it might have been a cutout of the surrounding dark. The two communed briefly and then the Doberman bounded out of the light and was gone, with Apple in his wake.

"Apple? Apple! Oh, you horrible animal," Amanda cried after her, and slammed the door.

Still, the dog had almost obeyed, and knew now that there was someone here to feed her. Even if she were safely inside, Amanda had decided at some point not to go home tonight. The prospect of waking and dressing Rosie, and then settling her all over again at the end of a fifteen-minute drive, would not have been appealing even in midsummer; as it was, the cold was daunting. Moreover, it would be far simpler to set out from here in the morning with a suitcase already packed to bring to the hospital.

". . . surrendered at shortly after noon today at the home of a brother. The other escapee is still at large," said the announcer. Amanda noticed for the first time that he was wearing a bow tie which had a clip-on air. "And now, a look at the weather. . . ."

She left the set on for the forecast. She looked in on Rosie, peacefully asleep with her knotted rag on the pillow beside her, and returned to wash her dinner utensils, not really listening yet because there was always a good three minutes of auctioneerlike babble about other places, including some handy information about the Dakotas and northern Michigan, preceding any word about the local weather. When she had turned off the faucet she stood still at the sink, blotting out the voice from the living room and trying to assess some subtle change in the house, or the night.

The wind had dropped with the abruptness of a switched-off electric fan; everything, including the cottonwood tree, was stilled. Did that mean a possibility of snow? Yes, said the announcer promptly; beginning after midnight, with an expected accumulation of two to four inches.

In a perverse way Amanda missed the wind, because now the silence of the house in which she was in charge of a fragile two-year-old had the quality of a blackboard which might be written upon at any moment. She thought uneasily that if she strained hard enough she might be able to hear leaves or buds in the plant room stirring in the moist dark, communicating with each other. In spite of the wholesome atmosphere which surrounded growing things, it was not a pleasant idea.

Distantly, the palomino whinnied, as if aware, too, of the altered fabric of the night. Amanda switched off the television set, found herself a novel, gave the telephone a resentful glance as she passed it. Why hadn't Justin, if in fact it had been Justin calling the Lopezes in search of her, tried her here, attempting, in this season of goodwill, to leave a message with her aunt?

The telephone remained silent for the time being. When it did ring, it wasn't Justin.

"You know, I think we might drift out of here and have some reviving Irish coffee at my place," said Lucy Pettit.

Justin was in hearty agreement with the first half of this proposal. There were two topics of discussion at the party: how Edie was taking the divorce and whether Max had really resigned from his highly paid public relations job or, as a majority seemed to think and hope, been fired. Justin was the only guest present not up on these matters—even Lucy had said to him disbeliev-ingly, "Oh, but you must know Max. Everybody does" —and whatever he had been drinking (punch, he was beginning to suspect) had given him a severe headache.

Although the headache might have had its real birth in the crash with which the poetry-reciting head-stander had suddenly overbalanced without warning. His nimble-looking sneakers had the impact of ski boots, and the leg of a coffee table had flown free, strik-ing the shin of an elderly woman in unguarded laven-dar chiffon. The magicians, true to their calling, had surveyed the shards of their cloisonné cigarette box and said with a kind of anguished imperturbality that it didn't matter at *all*, just so long as he hadn't hurt him-self.

Now, headache notwithstanding, Justin wanted to have another try at reaching Amanda while there was a telephone readily available. Mrs. Balsam must be home by now. He said to Lucy, "Will you cast an eye around for our hosts? I'll be right back," and began to thread his way through clusters of people to the room with the photographs and the caged doves.

Here he met with an obstacle. A blond woman as large and slippery as a walrus was seated at the desk, one hand firmly and protectively on the receiver. "I hope you don't want to use this," she said, "because I'm waiting for the New York operator to call back."

"No, that's all right," said Justin, and gave the doves a hypocritical greeting and withdrew. Wait? No. Long-distance circuits tended to busy around holidays, the blond woman looked implacable, the need for solid food was becoming imperative. Feeling manipulated by an unfriendly fate, he went in search of Lucy, the magicians, and, as soon as possible, the door.

*   *   *

49

"Mrs. Balsam?"

It was a woman's voice this time. Amanda, who had had time to reflect that Mrs. Balsam's situation was not a fleeting one and there might well be arrangements which she would want cancelled, said, "My aunt is in the hospital, I'm afraid. May I take a message for her?"

"Oh, I'm sorry to hear that." It was detached, perfunctory. "This is a neighbor, and I'm calling to say that her horse is out."

"*Again?*" Still, for Amanda, it had no significant echo. Horses got loose with frequency; on a number of occasions she had tethered one to a tree on her front lawn so that the cruising owners could locate it easily. "Thank you for letting me know. I wish I could go after her, but I can't right now."

There was a severe silence; she had sinned against a code. Horse owners got up at all hours in all weathers to retrieve animals who might cause property damage, or get a leg caught in a barbed-wire fence or fall and become wedged in a dry irrigation ditch.

"I don't know this area at all well," said Amanda doggedly, "and I have a very young child here whom I can't just leave."

There was another judgmental pause and then a very cool, final, "Well, it's her horse."

Amanda didn't like her. "As a matter of fact, it isn't," she said pleasantly, a fact which they both knew made Mrs. Balsam all the more responsible. "Where is the horse, in case I can get hold of someone to help?"

The directions sounded complicated, and she wrote them down: Take the left fork after the feed store and then another left; there was a dirt road which was really a private driveway, so skip that and continue about a quarter of a mile to a big field on the right. There were other horses there, and at last view the palomino had been standing under trees at the edge.

Amanda thanked the aloof voice and hung up distractedly. Drougette was a valuable mare and had been entrusted to Mrs. Balsam. Had that earlier whinny been by way of farewell? Or—all pale horses must look pretty much alike at night—was it Drougette at all?

She would have to go and see. She put on her coat, got the flashlight, went out again into the frigid dark.

The stars were gone. She walked in a moving pocket of stillness broken only by her own footsteps, and when she left the reflected glow from the house and switched on the flashlight a baby owl on a fence post subsided out of its feathers and glided away. Amanda felt as if she were emerging onto the blackest of stage sets, with countless eyes aware of her and some thunderclap thing to come.

No friendly shape stirred in the corral. It didn't need a strand-by-strand inspection of the wire, which she had no intention of making in this bone-piercing cold, to tell her that the mare had indeed found a way out.

For the first time, it occurred to her to wonder if her aunt had acquired an enemy without realizing it. Amanda had once declined an offer of yard work by three boys, explaining that she did it herself for exercise, and found the front seat of her car strewn with fiberglass the next morning. There was no proof that that had been a retaliatory gesture, even though the boys had stared at her in sullen disbelief, and there were horses who were escape artists. Still, twice in one week seemed odd, as Mrs. Balsam could not have enjoyed her after-dark expedition and would have taken steps to see that it did not happen again. Or maybe— Christmas week—she hadn't been able to get anyone and had simply done some amateur repairs herself and hoped for the best.

Call Justin, thought Amanda, returning to the house with a beleaguered impulse to cry. First the Afghan, now the mare. Rosie at least was here, switched over onto her other side, silky black hair straying across her face. Amanda tucked it gently back and closed the window.

She dialed Justin. She warned herself after the first two unanswered rings that he was not going to be home, so as to prepare herself, and it didn't help at all.

Up until seven o'clock that evening everything had been going well, with the ride East tomorrow arranged for Claude out of a mixture of bribes and threats. Sweet hadn't dared go near the Balsam house since delivering his half brother there the night before last, but Mrs. Balsam would be leaving as usual at one-thirty. Meanwhile, there was water in the shelter, and in his own kitchen Sweet had filled his pockets, after that frantic telephone call, with a welter of candy bars and boxes of raisins intended for the Christmas stockings of Teresa's nieces and nephews.

The police artist's sketch bore very little resemblance to Claude. He had gone too faithfully by the "flattened features" described by Beryl Green, which did not take into account a wide sharp mouth, and the other witness had overestimated Claude's height by nearly two inches.

In any case, cautious inquiries indicated that no one had come looking for Claude. There was no employer to wonder at his nonappearance for work. The news bulletins—and the Sweets' radio stayed on habitually from the time they woke in the morning until they went to bed—were beginning to emphasize the delay in getting a police car to the scene, and, tacitly, the probability that the fugitive and his captive had been out of the area before there was even an official report.

So far, so good, even though there were things that Sweet blocked out of his memory. Still, he had belatedly realized tonight that a lot of businesses closed at noon on Christmas Eve. Would Mrs. Balsam's? Easy enough to find out, by indirection; he would offer to come around tomorrow afternoon and measure for some shelves she wanted put up in her plant room.

The strange voice, belonging to the niece he hadn't even known existed, had given him a shock. On top of that, like a sustaining brick pulled out from under, Patch, provider of the ride—Sweet did not know his real name, but had reliable information about participation in a recent liquor store holdup—had telephoned to say tersely that his own plans had changed and it was tonight or not at all. Although he was unaware of his passenger's identity he was suspiciously take-it-or-leave-it, and Sweet had already pushed him to the limit.

To duplicate the action of two nights ago—setting the mare loose with a sharp spank and then making a lightning descent on Mrs. Balsam's house as soon as she had left it—seemed dangerous, but there wasn't time to arrange an alternative plan. There would soon be an even broader hue-and-cry, and Claude had to be out of the state, equipped with a blondish wig which Sweet had acquired yesterday, when it started.

Now, from above, he watched Mrs. Balsam's house, and waited. Teresa would have made her call about the mare ten minutes ago, but nothing was happening. There was a phone booth a mile and a half down the road, and after a further five minutes Sweet used it, and was stunned.

The fact that Mrs. Balsam was in the hospital could only mean that Claude had emerged from the shelter against all prohibitions, been discovered, and attacked her. Why hadn't there been anything in the news? Ellie Peale was very much on the public mind, and every incident of violence involving women was being closely scrutinized.

The niece was there in the house with a small child; there must be a way to turn that to advantage. On the other hand, Teresa had reported that she had said she might be able to get someone to help—Sweet assumed this to be a man—and he would have to watch a while for that.

He was cold at his vantage post. He was not nearly as cold as Ellie Peale.

Chapter 6

Amanda resettled herself purposefully with her book, discovering by page twenty-three that she was going to have to start all over again. It had begun with a fashionable funeral, but now she was looking at something incomprehensible about children gathering strawberries.

Her worry about Apple had largely dissipated—nothing much could happen to a dog under the escort of a full-grown Doberman pinscher—but Drougette was another matter. All else apart, what about the spectre of a wrongful-death suit? Very occasionally a car traveling at speed collided with a galloping horse, with disastrous results to all concerned. So far as Amanda could judge from the complex directions given to her by the woman caller and her own hazy notion of this area, the mare couldn't be more than a mile and a half away, but would she stay there, harmlessly nibbling at bark and enjoying the company of other horses?

She must, because it would be unthinkable to leave a sleeping two-year-old while she found a rope and drove off into the night with no idea of the extent of her mission; that was the kind of errand undertaken by the Judge Craters of the world. It was equally unthinkable to wake and dress her small charge and take her along on this bitter night. A developing chill which would be only a mild concern with another child could be perilous indeed for Rosie Lopez.

Was it possible that, even though she had been fed and watered so recently, Drougette might wander back to the corral by herself? If so, she had better find the gate open. Amanda put on her coat, stood for a moment while she pinned down an associated thought, and took her car keys from her handbag.

She couldn't remember locking her car, in her preoccupation over Mrs. Balsam, and although the chances were probably less than those of winning the Irish sweepstakes it had to be considered that there was an escaped convict still abroad, presumably looking for transport or (far worse) a place to lurk until morning and the emergence of the unsuspecting car owner.

From outside, there was a curious rushing, whomping sound. The timing was eerie, and Amanda snatched her hand back from the knob of the patio door and stayed riveted for long seconds before, nothing further ensuing, she opened the door and peered cautiously out.

A huge cottonwood limb, of killing weight to anyone standing inattentively under it, had been weakened by the earlier winds and taken its time about crashing down. After a little wary listening Amanda skirted it, undid the catch on the corral gate and propped it wide open, and proceeded around the house to her car.

She hadn't locked the driver's door. She shone the

flashlight in and used her key. The scrupulous person who had restored Mrs. Balsam's car keys to her handbag hadn't locked the Rabbit, and Amanda did that now; for some reason the slamming echoes seemed as sharply telltale as black footprints in new snow. She ran back the way she had come, the flashlight beam swinging brilliantly, but that was a mixture of cold and superstition. She had no sensation whatever of being watched.

She had now, as stoically as though she had actually reached him and been told that he was sorry he couldn't get away from wherever he was, given up on Justin, which meant that she had to close her mind to the problem of the palomino. There was no one else to whom she could say, at this hour, "Would you bring a rope and catch a horse for me?"

She had left her own telephone number at the hospital, not anticipating the night's turn of events, and although it was unlikely that they had tried to reach her she dialed.

"Would you hold on a minute, please, Miss Morley? I believe there's something—"

This could not be bad news, Amanda assured herself, still gripping the receiver in surprise because she had expected the stereotyped statement, and the alert voice was presently back. Mrs. Balsam had been sedated for the night, but earlier she had managed to speak. Just the one word—the nurse with her at the time thought it was "sell"—but she had said it more than once.

Sell the house, that would mean, thought Amanda when she had hung up. Well, that was only logical. Stroke victims sometimes recovered almost completely, but that would be a long process, and even though Mrs. Balsam had been left comfortably well-off and a part-time nurse could be arranged, the place where she had lain helpless and terrified would hold indelible memories.

Meanwhile, her terrible silence had been unlocked, however tinily; it must have been like a pinprick in an intolerable tension. As if some of the release extended to her too, Amanda took off the heels she had been wearing since seven-thirty that morning, padded down the hall, looked in at Rosie, and switched on a lamp in her aunt's bedroom.

It was attractive and tranquil, part sitting room as well, with a small desk and striped satin chair, a long bookcase under the big window which looked across a river of lights to the mountains, a comfortably tufted hassock. And, of course, the ubiquitous gray-blue carpeting.

Amanda drew the curtains and took off the very simple larkspur suit she had also worn all day. She was taller than her aunt, but one of the closets behind louvered doors yielded a robe which was wearable and a pair of slippers too small but backless. Hand on the light switch, she took it away in response to some fragmented suggestion from her brain, walked around the bed, pulled open the top middle bureau drawer.

Mrs. Balsam kept her casual jewelry in a sumptuous leather case nestled under scarves and stockings. The rest, including a diamond and sapphire dinner ring with matching earrings and a bracelet with alternating links of gold and emeralds, reposed in the inside pocket of an old raincoat with fraying cuffs. "I can't see going to the bank every time I want to wear something," she had told Amanda in explanation of this novel arrangement, "and as they'll be yours you ought to know where they are."

58

It was not quite the harebrained idea it might have seemed, because any rational burglar would have bypassed the kind of garment used for gardening in favor of a pale mink cape. And it was still working: When Amanda thrust a hand deep into the raincoat's pocket a palmful of sparkle came out.

What had she thought, if it was anything as organized as thought? That her aunt might unwittingly have left a door unlocked, and returned to her house for her letters to find some menacing stranger emerging from it? Been given a violent push, precipitating the stroke?

The ghost of personal attack was laid. Amanda switched off the lamp, closed the door of the guest room very softly because this part of the house was chilly with the window lowered there, and jumped at the loud imperative clatter of the door knocker.

There were people who habitually announced themselves in this fashion, as though come with foreclosure papers, and they were not as a rule likable people. Amanda called militantly through the crack, "Who is it?" and received a terse "Colonel Robinson" in reply.

An escaped convict could call himself anything he liked, and a military title would be a nice touch. Amanda, who had left the light on for Apple, opened the door a stingy two inches and then opened it wider at once.

A tall trim pink-skinned man stood there, close-clipped white head tipped back so as to gaze disfavorably down at her. Behind him, now haltered, was Drougette, looking, with her ashen forelock, like a fairy-tale animal of silver and gold. At the foot of the driveway, a car with its headlights on throbbed impatiently.

"I believe this is your horse," said the man without prelude.

"Yes." It wasn't a time for hairsplitting. "Thank you very much for bringing her back. Where did you—?"

"In my wife's bonsai garden," said the colonel uncompromisingly.

Those miniature trees, patiently trained into the staggery, asymmetrical shapes that appeared in Japanese prints, trampled happily under iron hooves. "I'm sorry," said Amanda, feeling shriveled. "I know my aunt, Mrs. Balsam, that is, will be glad to do whatever you think is fair. If you could just tether the horse to one of the car bumpers while I—" automatically, she indicated her robe and slippers "—I'll see that you get your halter back tomorrow."

But the colonel, expecting a woman of his own age, had taken approving inventory of the cream and green robe which on Amanda was not quite knee-length, and the copper-brown hair beginning to tendril out of its top-of-the-head knot. "If you can lend me a flashlight, I'll be glad to put her away for you."

It was nearly ten minutes before he knocked again, an interval during which the waiting car headlights snapped off with a suggestion of temper. "Wires were down at the northeast corner," he said, handing the flashlight back to Amanda, "but I've gotten them to hold at least for tonight. That's a beautiful mare, by the way."

Amanda renewed her thanks. "And about your wife's bonsai—"

"Unnatural damn little things," confided the colonel. "What did you say your name was?"

Amanda told him and he withdrew into the dark, pink and military but no longer parade ground. She closed and locked the door with the conviction that her immediate world was beginning to right itself. The Afghan was still at large, true, but Rosie slept snugly in the

60

guest room, Drougette had been returned without incident (or almost; how much did bonsai trees cost?) and was safely confined for the night; most importantly of all, her aunt had managed to speak.

Read for a while, because she was not an early retirer, and then give Apple one last call and go to bed. Amanda turned down the thermostat in preparation, propped pillows against one end of the couch, and stretched herself out.

Sitting in his pickup on a curve above the house, Sweet watched the disintegration of his plan.

This could not be the man the niece had hoped to enlist in the capture of the mare, which he had last seen cantering off into the dark. It was much too soon; the driver of the car had stayed in it; the white-haired man, visible in the light at the front door although Sweet could not see the woman inside, stood there less than a minute both times he appeared. This was the behavior of strangers rather than friends, neighborhood residents who had spotted the palomino, knew where it belonged, and, conscientious as most Southwesterners were in such matters, brought it back.

Which might mean there was someone else coming, someone to whom, after summoning him out on what had proved to be an unnecessary mission, the niece would be bound to offer coffee or a drink.

Patch would not wait past the appointed time; that was implicit. Enragingly, all Sweet needed in Mrs. Balsam's house was ten minutes, maybe less, and he and Claude would be safely out of there. A way had to exist, because the alternative . . .

He had been fingering his short woolly beard as he gazed concentratingly down at his objective; now, he dropped his hand as if it had burned him. The speculation as to whether Mrs. Balsam had died had been in the back of his mind ever since Teresa had relayed the information that she was in the hospital, but it was suddenly in the very forefront, bright and sharp.

He drove down the hill and away, reminding himself that although she retained possession of the house he had one strong advantage over the niece, because she was obviously unaware that she and the child were not alone in the house. When he had gone about a mile he passed a small abandoned church, and did not even turn his head.

The couch was extremely comfortable. After a little while Amanda sat up and appropriated Rosie's wool blanket; after a further interval, when pages of her book began to flip over as her eyelids dropped, she reached up behind her, discarded one of the propping cushions, turned off the lamp, and stretched out full length.

This was the kind of drowsiness that had an eggshell fragility at its onset; to break it now might be to invite hours of wakefulness later. The soft light from the hall did not penetrate here. Apple would come, presently, and Amanda could not fail to hear her, and *then* she would get up and wash her face and brush her teeth and crawl into the other guest room bed.

A feather of sound that would have been buried in the night's earlier wind brushed against the light beginning of sleep. It had a guarded quality which inanimate materials could not achieve, suggesting a muffled nudge, and it had not come from the deep interior of the house where Rosie slept. It had come from somewhere much closer than that.

Amanda sat up with instinctive caution, eyes roaming the darkness which was not quite absolute, and dropped instantly, soundlessly back, because she had seen what must have sent that crippling roar of blood to Mrs. Balsam's brain.

Chapter 7

A human shape was growing impossibly up out of the floor to the side of the kitchen, moving black against almost-black stillness.

Amanda, her own heartbeats tumbling, pressed herself tightly into the couch, as immobilized and nearly as will-less as a rabbit at the stooping approach of a hawk. It seemed to her that her presence was stamped all over the dark, and that at any moment, at the end of a mincing prowl down the step and across the room, a pair of hands would come thrusting over the back of the couch.

The pulse of blood in her ears at this incarnation of all the unrecognized fears of childhood had made her briefly deaf. Gradually, she became aware of an infinitely careful progress which was not so much sound as the flawing of silence, and then a tiny, trembly vibration.

A gulp of light registered faintly on the living room

ceiling. The shape risen from the floor—a man, said Amanda's bared senses—had opened the refrigerator door.

Infinitesimal click as glass touched glass, tremor of metal as something was slid across a shelf: Amanda realized that in the guest room she would have heard none of this; she would have been peacefully asleep.

And she should not have thought that, because as if she had sent some desperate mental signal a breathy little voice called anxiously, "Manda?"

Dear God. Rosie stirring, turning, discovering that the broad friendly shaft of light over the end of her strange bed was gone, coming now in all innocence to betray Amanda. Would she venture into alien darkness on her tottery little legs? Amanda clenched her hands helplessly—and Rosie had advanced along the hall.

"Manda?" Subdued, but growing frightened.

The dim light vanished as the refrigerator door was pressed rubberily shut. This time the almost soundless progress was swift, and it was unmistakably flight. The muffled nudge that had halted Amanda's slide into sleep was repeated, this time with finality.

Silence, broken by Rosie's first forlorn sob. Amanda eased herself off the couch, whispering, "Here I am, Rosie," even before she tiptoed across the rug and into the dimming wash of gold at the doorway. She picked up the child, blessing the quality of voice which would have led the man to believe that it was addressing someone a safe distance away, and went swiftly into the guest room.

Her heart had steadied somewhat, because that monstrous black shape—for the moment at least—had been as frightened of discovery as she, but her hands shook badly over the dressing of Rosie; had her tiny clothes really contained all these buttonholes before? She

66

thought disconnectedly that if she were required to sign her name right now she couldn't, with any kind of legibility.

In fact, she was having trouble with simple shoelaces. "We're going to my house just as soon as I get dressed, Rosie. Come on. . . ."

She couldn't drive in these ill-fitting slippers, and she had probably used up less than a minute and a half with all her fumbling. Going fast and very quietly into her aunt's bedroom, she flung off the robe and got into her suit, misbuttoning the jacket, and put on her shoes. It came as a scald to realize that her coat and handbag were still in the living room along with Rosie's blanket, so that she had to go back into that violated darkness— and that the telephone was ringing like an alarm bell.

Amanda stood paralyzed. Answer it and breathe an urgent message, at the same time publishing to the undoubtedly listening man the fact that there was someone awake and knowledgeable here? How far would she get before he exploded out of hiding at her?

"The telefoam," whispered Rosie in reproach, and Amanda whispered back, "But we won't answer it."

This drew the wonderful, abashed, nobody-knows-but-us smile; still, it seemed a nerve-fraying eternity before the ringing stopped. He would be convinced now, wouldn't he, that that very small and distant voice had retired into sleep again?

Which would of course, realized Amanda, thunderstruck, embolden him to re-emerge from what could only be the cellar and continue his interrupted exploration of the refrigerator. *Cellar.* That was what Mrs. Balsam had been straining to say, that was the warning in her mutely burning stare at Amanda's announced intention of coming here tonight, that was behind all her terror. She hadn't even known that she owned a cellar, imcomprehensible though that was; had said when she sold some of the furniture from the bigger house in the Heights, "I'd keep some of these things if I had any storage space at all."

And then to see through the window a man materializing out of the floor at the end of her kitchen, making a mockery of locks and keys—

A trapdoor, thought Amanda, trying to take some of the horror out of this. And—not fleeing when the coast was clear that afternoon, but returning to his underground habitat—he must be the escaped convict, bafflingly possessed of a fact which Mrs. Balsam did not know, biding his time until the police hunt had slackened in intensity.

A man who had made that bid for freedom, and been successful so far, would be very alert to the possibility of danger with someone demonstrably awake during his venture up into the kitchen. Amanda deliberately did not think of him listening, concentrating, just under the floor. Instead, she placed in her mind the exact location of her handbag with the all-important car keys: on the end table with the two stamped letters which had triggered this whole situation.

She whispered imperatively to Rosie, "Stay here, I'll be right back," and tiptoed down the hall and into the living room. Her heart began a helpless acceleration, because after the lighted glow of the bedroom it was like entering a black cave which might or might not contain an animal with its head up, sniffing. She skirted the end of the couch, trying to walk weightlessly, remembered that there was an armchair at an oblique angle to it a few feet away, negotiated that passage, put her hand cautiously out and down.

A pottery ashtray rocked sharply on wood, and it was all Amanda could do not to sob like Rosie, and then her

68

fingers touched leather. She seized the handbag, turned with a little more certainty, gathered up her coat and then the plaid blanket as she passed the couch again, had to be careful to confine herself to a walk because even this carpeting wouldn't drink up all vibration and they wouldn't be safe until they were in the car with the doors locked and the engine running.

Rosie was sitting obediently on the hassock in Mrs. Balsam's bedroom, her eyes round with bemusement. Amanda plucked her car keys out of her bag, dropped them into her coat pocket for easy location in the dark, and deployed the blanket with a reassuring smile. "Here we go," she said, and lifted the child and tiptoed to the patio door.

Apple was there, wagging her tail in greeting, and this time her companion was not a Doberman pinscher.

The restaurant was the blackest Justin had ever been in, punctuated by orange-shaded table lamps which created an impression of lights at sea. He held Lucy's arm firmly, and not only because of the leg-breaking obscurity which contained two steps down. "You'll feel better when you've had some food," he said.

"Oh, but all those cheese and crackers," said Lucy vaguely, being seated with some difficulty.

One cheeseless cracker, Justin remembered, because when the female magician had finally produced a platter of stuffed olives and cubes of Cheddar and crackers there had been what amounted to a genteel stampede. The wounded woman in lavendar chiffon had been helped to a good deal, solicitously. The sneakered man responsible for the navy-blue bump on her shin and the coffee table propped up with books had discreetly vanished.

The menu here was written on the label of a jug in

trembly and indecipherable script, and as Justin peered at it without success a waiter arrived, jaunty in patched jeans. "Something from the bar, sir?" he offered alertly, observing Lucy's lolling head.

"Just something to eat, at the moment. What's quickest?"

The waiter said with disdain that there was a chef's salad with julienne—

"We'll have that," said Justin summarily. "Where is the telephone?"

He was told. He said to Lucy, "Will you be all right while I make a quick call?" and, upon her glassy assent, picked his way through the midnight gloom to the single booth at the back.

A fat man in a tiny Tyrolean hat was in possession. Justin, normally civilized in such matters, patrolled mercilessly back and forth because his need to hear Amanda's voice suddenly outstripped his need for food. Where was she, two nights before Christmas? (Well, where was he? Out with Lucy Pettit. Amanda wouldn't be able to reach him if, undone by the sentiments of the season, she tried. In which case, in any case, the thing to do was demolish the salad, drop Lucy off at her apartment with all possible speed, and go home and listen to his telephone not ringing.)

The fat man emerged from the booth, staring hard and unpleasantly at Justin, who said, "Sorry, urgent matter," and took his place. He tried his trio of numbers again, letting Mrs. Balsam's ring the longest in case she had gone to bed, but nobody was home anywhere.

Examine this. Was he suddenly determined on Amanda out of a sophomoric whim, merely because she was unavailable? No. There was nothing sophomoric about his feeling for Amanda.

The salad had arrived in his absence. Lucy was gaz-

70

ing at hers oddly. Justin said encouragingly, "This looks very good," and used salt and a pepper grinder the size of a young pillar. He lifted his fork, although he was almost hungry enough to do without one, and Lucy, forehead glistening ominously, said, "Justin, you will have to get me out of here. I mean right now, this minute."

There was no mistaking her; equally, there wasn't time to try to break the secret code on the jug. Justin put down too much money for a pair of chef's salads no matter who the chef was, said briefly to the waiter who accosted them suspiciously in the murk a few moments later, "We've paid. You will rue any delay, believe me," and made it outside with Lucy, just.

"My name is Peter Dickens," said the man on Mrs. Balsam's patio, "and I live—" he cocked his head at a far twinkle of lights "—over there. I don't know whether you've been listening to the radio, but I thought the lady who lives here ought to know that a man's been seen in the neighborhood who they think—"

"He's here in this house, in the cellar," blurted Amanda uncontrollably, because—open-featured, clean-shaven, reliably clad in a fawn raincoat over a dark blue blazer and slacks—this was exactly the kind of neighbor who would stop by with a friendly warning. "I don't know how he got in, but I saw him not ten minutes ago and I'm on my way home to call the police. Thank you anyway. Apple—"

"We can save time by calling the police from here," interrupted the man. He had very clear candid blue eyes, and in some way, without actually brushing past her, he was starting to enter the house.

"No, thanks," said Amanda sharply and with feeling.

"I'm not staying here a second longer."

She stepped forward, forcing him back, pressing in the lock button on the knob so that she could close the door safely behind her. She was unprepared for the gloved finger that came up to tickle Rosie under the chin. "Cute," said the man. "Is she yours?"

There was something very wrong about this swift transition from the courteously helpful to the personal. There was also something wrong about the glove, skin-fitting and semitransparent. "Good night," said Amanda, cool with a tremendous effort; she was just beginning to realize what she had done by her impetuosity. This was a menace related to the one inside, because no well-intentioned stranger would come to the side door of a house which looked from the road as if its occupant had retired for the night. Would he have forced his way in if she hadn't obligingly turned the knob for him?

And the Afghan, she thought, stomach tightening with fear, had all the protection value of a canary. She said, "Excuse me," attempting again to get by him, and his teeth flashed whitely at her.

"Excuse *me,*" he said, and like lightning, before there could be any question of a struggle, he had taken Rosie from her and walked into the house.

Because no voices had been raised, Rosie, handed frequently about from nurses to doctors in her short life, simply peered back with wildly questioning eyes. "It's all right, Rosie," Amanda managed, and followed, closing the door.

She had turned out the hall light earlier, and something warned her hand away from the switch. In the faint reflected glow from the patio it was still an astonishment to her that this safe-looking man was actually holding Rosie. She said in a steady voice, preserving the strange calm, "If that—the other one has to get away, he can have my car keys and what cash there is in the house."

She suspected as she spoke that the offer was useless, but it had to be made. "Get me a scarf," said the man unheedingly.

And now there was no doubt about it: His was the voice which had been surprised at hers on the telephone. Amanda, going instantly into her aunt's bedroom because as long as he had possession of Rosie she would have to do as she was told, thought she knew what the scarf was for. "I saw him," she had said in that first disastrous impulse, but from the panic in her manner and the fact that she was there at all, clearly poised for flight, it had been a fast glimpse, unreciprocated. She wasn't to be allowed another look at the man in the cellar. Rosie, of course, did not count as a witness at all.

Still, how did he dare let her out from under his eye, even with a child as hostage? Many Southwesterners—Amanda guessed a predominance—kept a firearm in the house, for hunting or target practice or self-defense. She did not, out of a fell conviction that before she could bring herself to squeeze the trigger the weapon would have been snatched away and turned against her, and neither did Mrs. Balsam, but how could he be sure that she would not emerge from the bedroom with a revolver or a rifle?

He knew the house, or Mrs. Balsam, or both.

He knew the house very well indeed. He had been able to put his hand on the key to the bedroom door almost without pausing, because the lock had just clicked decisively.

Amanda, at the bureau, dropped folds of navy chiffon back and ran to the door, recognizing belatedly the pecularly unburdened feeling of her left wrist. The handbag she had slung there after picking up Rosie had been dislodged by that swift maneuver over the child.

She wrenched at the doorknob in spite of the evidence of her ears. Mouth against the crack, she called, "Please, won't you at least let her in here with me?"

Silence; Rosie must still be too bewildered, or by now too frightened, to cry. She was to be the guarantee of good behavior on Amanda's part while the man in the cellar was spirited out of the house. They wouldn't, would they, take her with them as a continuing safeguard?

Remembered television and newspaper scenes shot dementedly through Amanda's head, of babies being used as living shields; with guns at their heads; being held threateningly over the edges of rooftops. Her hands were gripped together so fiercely that they hurt. She relaxed them, drew a few deep shaky breaths, left the door briefly to turn on the bedside clock radio to a thread of sound.

By this time the police would have done a thorough canvassing of the remaining escapee's relatives and friends; mightn't that have led them to the man who called himself Peter Dickens? But how could they ever connect him to Mrs. Balsam's house? (And if only she had said to him, at the patio door, "Thank you, but my aunt is away and I'm just leaving," she and Rosie would be on the road to home right now.)

That did not bear thinking about. Music came on, and from its nature this was the station that had news breaks at frequent intervals. Amanda went back to the door again. Now there was a faint neutral sound, which might have been someone talking steadily or water running at full force; it seemed to have no variation.

The music stopped, and a woman disk jockey said

74

smoothly, "Wasn't that pretty? Oh-hhh, my. At the top of the local news, the second of two state penitentiary escapees at large for nearly forty-eight hours has been captured by police. That bulletin just in, no details as yet. In the search for Ellie Peale, the clerk abducted from a convenience store also two nights ago, a Corrales man was questioned but has been released. State Representative David Esquibel, under pressure because of his stand on wilderness—"

Amanda's shocked hand went out and snapped the radio voice into silence. Who, then, did the cellar hide? A man with an even more desperate need for sanctuary because he had taken a young girl with whose face the whole city was now familiar? Had Amanda herself, earlier, been pan-broiling steak and mushrooms and tomatoes obliviously while under her feet Ellie Peale was being prevented from crying out? Or could no longer cry out?

Quivira Road, the location of the convenience store, was a good eight miles away. This house was isolated, and two nights ago Mrs. Balsam had been summoned out of it because the palomino mare was loose. Set loose? With another decoy call tonight?

Amanda moved on trembling legs to the bedroom door. From the other part of the house was the sound of a sudden sharp impact, and now, at last, Rosie began to cry.

Chapter 8

As of late that afternoon, there was one fresh piece of information in the background of the Peale case. It was far from reassuring.

The girl's mother and stepfather had disapproved strongly of her working at the Speedy-Q because of the late hours and the vulnerability of such places, and it was to a high-school friend since moved to Denver that Ellie had confided by letter certain drawbacks to her new job. The Denver papers had carried the story of her abduction in capsule form, because it was possible that she had been transported over a state line, and the friend, Joanne Faber, had seen it on her return from a skiing vacation and telephoned the Albuquerque police.

What she had to report wasn't much, but it was sinister. Early in December Ellie had written to say that she had an admirer who gave her the creeps by cruising up in a van, usually at about ten or ten-thirty, and simply parking there and staring into the store. He was always alone. In a following letter he had come inside, not to buy anything but to ask her for a date.

Here, where there should have been physical details, there were none, but Ellie Peale could not have known how important they would be. Joanne Faber still had the letter, and read from it: " 'He's really weird. He reminds me of George Anderson, remember him?' "

Again, what sounded promising was not. Joanne Faber explained that the only memorable feature of this boy had been his preoccupied way of crossing the high-school campus, so that when he tripped or bumped into other students he never looked down or back to see what had caused the impediment to his progress.

Singleminded, indrawn, taking no heed of obstacles in his path. It brought back memories of a case, a dozen years ago but vivid in its unpleasantness, in which a quiet, bespectacled sophomore, after admiring a classmate from afar for most of a semester, had waylaid the girl a half mile from her home, made unsuccessful advances, beaten her to death with a brick and buried her body. The psychiatric report had said, "Inability to cope with real or imagined rejection," which to the people who had to deal with the results seemed something of an understatement.

They were dealing here with weeks instead of months, but also with a man instead of a boy. In view of the unbalanced nature of the act, and the time elapsed, the prospects for Ellie Peale did not look bright.

On the other hand, the police now had hold of a slender thread. The convenience store would have its regular customers, people living nearby who depended on it for cigarettes or a loaf of bread, and someone must

78

have been curious about the frequently parked van with its single occupant. It was true that no one had come forward in spite of the extensive television and newspaper coverage of the case and the appealing quality of the girl herself, but the number of people who said defensively, "Well, I wasn't sure," or "I might be getting an innocent person in trouble" or even, "Nobody asked me," was astonishing.

In the morning, concentrate on that.

"There must be something here, goddamn it!"

Claude had convinced himself that there would be penicillin or an equivalent in the refrigerator; finding none, he spun and hurled a jar of mustard shatteringly against the far living room wall. The shelf from which he had taken it looked as though it had been pawed by a foraging bear. The terrified Afghan bounded up on the couch to seek protection from the small child who, unnerved by the explosion of glass and not at all sure of the large dog's intentions, began to cry.

"Get it clean for now," said Sweet economically. He had filled the steel sink with scaldingly hot water while the other man used the electric shaver he had brought, and produced a cake of soap from the cabinet beneath. "There'll be an all-night drugstore on the way. Hurry up, Claude. This guy won't wait."

His half brother, startlingly transformed by the neat, deep-blond wig concealing the dark hair he had had trimmed for Ellie Peale's benefit, turned a face suffused with rage and pain but plunged his hand wincingly into the sink. Sweet, his jaw feeling naked, walked down into the living room and confronted the wailing child on the couch. "You shut up," he said with ferocity.

Rosie, who had never before been spoken to with real menace, understood at once and subsided into jerky,

79

wide-spaced gasps. Sweet was uneasy with children at the best of times, and this specimen, with her tiny monkey face and big dark eyes, made him more nervous than most. He presented his back to her while he cut the telephone cord, then gave his attention to Mrs. Balsam's navy blue handbag on top of a bookcase. Her car keys were in it; he pocketed them.

Was it possible that she was dead? Claude swore that he hadn't touched her, hadn't even seen her, and he was obviously telling the truth. But heart attacks could come on without warning, and it was those nimble types who suddenly dropped in their tracks while the ones with whole lists of ailments tottered on forever.

The other set of car keys that mattered were in the handbag he had yanked off the niece's wrist. Not replying to the hammering on the bedroom door, or the cried "If you've hurt that child— She isn't well, can't you see that?" Sweet walked silently to the patio door, picked up the bag, returned with it to the living room. Under Rosie's terrified stare, ignoring the timid advances of the dog who had had a kick aimed at her by Claude, he went rapidly through its contents.

The keys weren't there; the girl must have them in a pocket, as he had tested both cars on his arrival and found them locked. Was it important? Sweet didn't think so. There were other ways of preventing her from getting to a telephone too soon.

Claude appeared, jacket-cuff refastened, forearm held away from his body in a gingerly curve. Sweet scooped all the coins out of the niece's change purse, shook the bag for any betraying clink of metal from the bottom, and said briefly, "Get in the truck."

Claude gazed uneasily at the couch. "What about the kid?"

80

"She goes in the bedroom. As asked. Will you for Christ's sake—"

Claude went out the front door fast, closing it behind him. Sweet walked to the couch and picked up the flinching, recoiling, corduroy-clad little figure. "I'm not going to hurt you," he said, because he did not want the niece flying at him in response to panicked screams; he had involved himself in trouble enough.

The encounter under the patio light had been una-voidable, with time running out, but Sweet thought he could survive it easily. It was conceivable that he had been taken note of while working on Mrs. Balsam's corral, but the blazer and slacks which Teresa had nagged him into buying, plus the raincoat, created a very different effect. With his beard shaved off he looked younger and more diffident. The niece could describe him to police as Anglo, average height, with brown hair and blue eyes, but how many men in the surrounding area, let alone the city, must that image cover?

And within a little more than two hours, Claude safely delivered to Patch and on his way out of the state, he and Teresa would be in Ojo Caliente with a swarm of her relatives who would swear if questioned that he had been there all evening.

He said evenly to the bedroom door, "I'm going to put the kid in there, so don't give me any trouble and don't come out for fifteen minutes."

He turned the key in the lock, opened the door just wide enough to thrust the child through, closed it again and, covered by the girl's frantically relieved, "Rosie. Don't worry, everything's all right," relocked the door soundlessly. He knew where almost everything was in this house, and before he followed Claude out into the dark he collected a wooden-handled knife with a sharp three-inch blade.

"He *frew* a thing," said Rosie, gathered up into safe arms, and Amanda, immeasurably grateful for this slight, warm weight, said, "But he's gone, and he won't come back."

Had she heard the very faint echo of the heavy front door a minute or two earlier, the departure of what she somehow was sure was the object-thrower, the black shape from the cellar? She waited tensely, and had to strain for the second exit: The man in the raincoat was quieter.

The car keys seemed to burn in her pocket, but victims of bank robberies usually obeyed their staying injunctions. Still listening to the night, Amanda put on Rosie's socks, neglected before in her wild haste; the car would be bitterly cold at first, with every square inch of clothing a help. She was presently rewarded by the purring vibration of an engine, dimming, vanishing.

Only nine minutes had gone by, but she went at once to the bedroom door. It remained firmly locked.

Briefly and nonsensically—as if she could ever have trusted him in the first place,—Amanda's eyes filled with tears at the perfidy of this. He was away in his car; he must have a continuing plan for his fugitive friend; he would undoubtedly have done something to the telephone, so why . . . ? Was he, in spite of her assurance to Rosie, intending to come back?

The Afghan, who did not like being alone when she knew there was company to be had, whimpered throatily at the door. Amanda said distractedly, "No, Apple," and turned and looked around her.

Two hours ago—was it only that?—she had found

this room tranquil and attractive. Now, seen through a fast blur which had to be blinked away, it might have adopted that appearance for purposes of entrapment. The two rectangular windows facing the road and set high in the wall on either side of the bed could not possibly be gotten through. The picture window opposite was flanked with narrow ones which levered out, but because of the contour of the land there was a drop. Amanda could maneuver herself through, but not holding Rosie; the child would have to jump.

And if she were too frightened to jump, Amanda would have to fumble her way through the dark to the corral for bales of alfalfa on which to stand.

She could hear her own unnatural breathing—gasp, hold, exhale. She longed for one of her increasingly rare cigarettes, but there wasn't time even if any had been at hand. She threw back the bed coverlet, stripped off the top blanket, folded it, crossed to one of the flanking windows. And discovered that the screens were still in place.

"Oh, *God!*" she said fiercely aloud, and that was a mistake; it made an instant hole in her precarious self-possession.

The top wing nut holding the screen turned easily. The bottom one would not. At the other window the screen seemed destined to stay in place until the end of time, without tools. Amanda ran to the bureau, searched its top in vain for manicure scissors or tweezers or any other implement, and wrenched open the middle drawer. Perhaps among the jewelry in the leather case?

Fingers shaking because the hands on the bedside clock seemed to be picking up speed, she snatched out a pair of Zuni bracelets with tapering silver ends. The coral one was too thick to fit into the bottom nut's narrow slot; the turquoise worked.

Amanda removed the screen, cranked the window open, pulled the tufted hassock into place, and stood Rosie on it. She said intensely, "We have to go home, Rosie, and the door doesn't work so we have to use this window. I'll go out first, and then you sit here—like this —and let go when I tell you and I'll catch you. I won't drop you, I promise." She searched the small face with its remains of tears, not liking to use this particular prod, knowing that she had to. "Will you do that? We don't like those men."

Rosie nodded transfixedly. Amanda edged the hassock a little to one side, dropped the blanket out, and found that her coat was hindering. She unbuttoned it and flung it after the blanket, got one leg out and then the other, after some difficult pivoting, and dropped into the dark, only guessing where the ground was.

Her right ankle received a bolt of fire, and she had to steady herself against the house, head down, before she could bend awkwardly for her coat and put it on. She thought at first that the pain had dizzied her, but the night was actually in motion. The snow predicted for midnight had arrived ahead of schedule.

Although the window sill wasn't more than six inches above her upreached arms, she was sharply worried about this unavoidable separation from the small creature inside the house. She called, "Rosie?" with a quickening of alarm, and the child appeared almost at once, one arm adorned with the Zuni bracelets. She was gazing down with solemn interest, her fear apparently forgotten in bemusement at these strange goings-on.

"Hold on tight, and sit down where I showed you," instructed Amanda.

Slowly, doubtfully, Rosie obeyed. Amanda positioned herself, already braced for the shock to her throbbing ankle. "Now let go, Rosie." She took an encouraging grip on the corduroyed legs. "Let yourself fall out."

To her disbelief, Rosie wagged her head. Even with the light behind her it was possible to see her confiding smile, her conviction that this was their private joke, that no adult would really expect her to do the kind of thing she had always been expressly forbidden.

Was the man who had snatched her from Amanda heading for the driveway right now? It would be far too dangerous to give a sudden yank at the dangling and bird-like legs. Amanda said in her steeliest voice, "Let go, Rosie. I'm not going to tell you again."

Either because this was the Lopezes' ultimate threat, or because she was taken off balance by the stern unfriendliness of someone she trusted, Rosie came plummeting in such a wildly neck-clasping fall that Amanda staggered briefly. Her ankle roared with pain. She gathered up the blanket, wrapped it envelopingly around her charge, and went past the end of the house at a limping run.

No night with snow on the ground was completely black, even to eyes dazzled by fierce concentration on a lighted window. Here was the driveway, clearly delineated, and there was her car, parked behind Mrs. Balsam's. The very fact of escape so near seemed to tempt a sudden rocketing of headlights with someone dangerous behind them, and Amanda, terrified of dropping the keys, had trouble locating the lock.

But the door was finally open and Rosie in her cocoon of blanket deposited on the passenger seat. With the door closed and the button pushed down, a kind of trembling reaction, almost a lassitude, set in; for a few moments Amanda simply sat. Then, foot placed high on the accelerator, hoping to take most of the strain with her heel, she started the car, switched on her lights, set the wipers moving on the furred windshield. The snow fell straight and thick, a soundless white downpour.

Back in a fast arc; in fact, speed all the way home: The sooner she saw a policeman the better. She was not going to accomplish either. The car, pleasantly responsive since its major tune-up a month ago, bumped sluggishly in reverse like something waked out of a profound sleep in a junkyard.

For the second time in less than twenty minutes, Amanda came close to tears. She had never gotten around to buying a flashlight for the glove compartment because she seldom drove at night, but there were matches there. She got out of the car and circled it. All the tires had been slashed; they were not only flat but puddled.

Set out for that distant glimmer of light on foot, in the snow, carrying Rosie in the slipping blanket, with her ankle biting her at every step? As if by way of firm advice, the light blinked off. Even in its damaged state, even if there might be steering problems, the car would be transport for at least a while, and shelter and a measure of protection as well. Once she was past this lonely stretch of road there would be a chance of meeting other cars, although it was getting late, and if she drove with her emergency flashers on and sounded her horn—

Not long ago, in a horrifying newspaper story, a man whose wife was in the throes of a heart attack on the seat beside him had done just that, finally and desperately driving on the wrong side of a divided highway, and nobody had paid any attention at all. Amanda forced that out of her mind, got back into the car, and, with difficulty, clanked and ground out of the driveway and onto the road.

Chapter 9

The rendezvous with Patch was set for an extensive and usually crowded parking lot which had been chosen because it was a midway point and not the natural habitat of any of the people concerned. Nor was it, by the same token, routine police territory.

The restaurant to which the lot belonged had once been a hacienda. Curved fireplaces in its interconnecting dining rooms, warmly white-walled, burned piñon wood from October to May. A guitar player occasionally prowled through. A reasonably wretched dinner could be had for ten dollars and a good one for fourteen, and such was the atmosphere that most diners, queried by one of the New York–bred owners as to the satisfactoriness of their meal, replied cravenly that the lukewarm, oversauced, and undernourished cannelloni was fine; delicious, really.

The prices served a double purpose in convincing relatives, out-of-town guests, and business connections that they were being treated handsomely and at the same time excluding any unwanted element. This was not a place for beer-chased whiskey or arguments which were settled with knives, and the two bartenders had never been called upon to do anything but produce drinks.

Sweet had driven as though he carried high explosives, in spite of his half brother's altered appearance, but it was still only three minutes after the appointed hour when he swung the pickup into the parking lot and cruised slowly through in apparent search of a convenient space. A light blue 1975 Camaro, Patch had said, but although the yellow arc light tended to distort colors it was clearly not there.

Patch, a careful, uncommunicative man with pressing reasons of his own for departing the state tonight, would have allowed for it but it was still a delaying factor. Sweet pulled up into the shadow of a giant spruce, said, "He'll be along any minute," to himself as well as to Claude, and took bills from his wallet and handed them across. "You've got Eddie Garcia's address. This ought to keep you until . . . "

He was forced to let that drop. Claude, taking the money without acknowledgment and folding it awkwardly into the front pocket of his jeans, was a capable enough auto mechanic—but not with a badly infected right hand. The way he held the hand away from him suggested fear and loathing as well as a guard against any jarring contact. He had always been something of a hypochondriac, and now he was crouched like an animal in shock.

A group of people emerged from the restaurant, the women giving little shrieks at the sight of the snow and proceeding to pick their way on tiptoe. Another three minutes had passed, and Sweet was suddenly and furiously sure of what had happened. Patch, never enthusiastic about this plan, had come early, waited until the hands on his watch stood in exact position, sped away. Still—

"Be right back," said Sweet abruptly, and got out of the truck into the falling snow. He looked quite at home here, with his confident carriage and air of brisk purpose; he might have been a patron going back to retrieve his wife's gloves.

Along with a few brilliant ojos and a long display case of Indian jewelry, the lobby contained a telephone booth. Sweet dropped in two of the dimes taken from the girl's purse—with all her change confiscated she could do him no harm at the crossroads booth if and when she escaped from the bedroom—and dialed.

Patch's number rang vainly. Either his wife had gone to stay with friends or relatives during his absence or Patch, anticipating his unencumbered getaway and Sweet's reaction to it, had instructed her not to answer.

Sweet slammed the receiver onto its rest, contrived a civil smile for the white-haired woman who glanced at him from behind the display case, and walked out into the snow again, his mind roaming and ranging. Like most manipulators, he had a nimble and fertile brain, a natural talent for turning events to his own use —but only when the initial scheme was his to begin with. This dangerous mess, far removed from his familiar world of casual thievery and double-dealing and intermittent involvement with drugs, had been thrust upon him with no warning whatever.

Fleetingly and for the first time, he saw his protective attitude toward Claude over the years for the near-fear it actually was. The effort not to look further at this had a steadying effect, and by the time he reached the truck he had said to himself that the current situation con-

89

tained two men, a girl, and a child too young to give any kind of testimony.

Wasn't there, if he moved fast, a workable equation here?

"*I'll* find it, thank you," said Lucy Pettit haughtily of the apartment key for which she had been rummaging unsuccessfully. She snatched her bag away from Justin's offered hand and, before he could stop her, upended it over her snowy doorstep.

A considerable number of objects plopped into the furry white, the smaller and harder ones disappearing at once. Justin bent and ruffled through the snow, Lucy meanwhile anchoring herself to the doorknob with an occasional outward weave, and retrieved two sets of keys and a wallet; anything else, he thought a trifle punitively, could if necessary await the spring thaw.

By means of an impulsive detour on the way here he had established that Amanda's house was dark, as was the Lopezes', and her car gone. He had now begun to think that Mrs. Balsam's telephone might be out of order, and it would be reassuring to drive up there, snow or no snow; very possibly there would be lights still on, and Amanda's car might even be parked in front. He knew this sudden quest to be irrational, even obsessive, but there it was.

First he had to get Lucy settled. It was she who had persuaded Justin to the magicians' party, but he could scarcely leave her in a condition to fall or otherwise harm herself. It was a wonder, he thought as he maneuvered her inside, that the living room didn't shock her sober: It was all creams and whites except for an abstract painting in pink and pimento red, a burnt orange butterfly chair, a daffodil lampshade over a base of Prussian blue.

90

Lucy sat instantly down in the orange chair and gazed dazedly at the table beside it. When Justin asked, "Will you be all right, Lucy? Will you go straight to bed?" she said, "Certainly," and attempted to light a white cigarette filter with a match.

This seemed to bring her situation home to her. Her eyes brimmed. "You can't wait to be rid of me."

"Don't be silly. That was deadly stuff we drank, and I think the best—"

"I don't blame you. I am des-pic-able," said Lucy, triumphing over the syllables while tears rolled down her cheeks. "I have made a, oh, what is it, a spectacle of myself. I am drunk. All I ask, and I don't think it's much asking, is a cigarette. Or would that be too much for Justin Howard? I don't like your name, by the way."

She was fast progressing from self-abasement to abuse. Justin gave her a cigarette and lit it, weighing what to do next. If he made her coffee, would it alert her just enough to wander around after he had left instead of going to bed, conceivably setting the apartment on fire? Even if she had sleeping pills they shouldn't be taken on top of liquor in spite of an emptied stomach.

On the other hand, he couldn't stay here all night. He went into the kitchen, investigated the refrigerator, and said robustly, "How about a beer?"

Beer was nourishment of a sort and, at this stage of the game, a soporific. Lucy turned in her chair and craned at him, a long suspicious stare. "Are you going to have one?"

"Yes," lied Justin. He opened a cabinet, took down a tall glass so that the beer should appear more enticing, poured, and carried it into the living room. "Here you are."

Lucy studied the glass profoundly, bringing it up to

eye level as though inspecting for minnows, and gave a strange contemptuous little smile. Justin thought for a second that she was going to empty it onto the rug; instead, she drank thirstily, set the glass down with great care, and looked at one of his hands and then the other. "I don't see yours."

"I'll go get it."

The mere notion of nourishment had set off gnawing hunger pains in Justin's long-neglected stomach. He returned to the refrigerator and glanced ravenously in. His hostess was extraordinarily slender, and small wonder: Here in the nondrinkable line were capers, horseradish, a solitary egg, a head of lettuce, a poisonous-looking yellow mixture in a dish, and an eggplant.

He thought wistfully of the salad over which his fork had hovered so briefly; he reflected even more poignantly that Amanda, a cheese-fancier, would have Port du Salut or Camembert or both. He closed the refrigerator door and looked in despair for crackers. There were none—but here, folded tightly and thriftily in its wrapper on one corner of the counter, was a heel of whole-wheat bread. Justin undid it with speed. She must have been saving it for some irritating bird; it was richly starred through with blue mold.

"Justin?" Very small voice; Lucy had veered again. "I'm sorry I said I didn't like your name. It was insec—inesk—I shouldn't have said it."

"That's all right, I didn't pick it out," Justin assured her, and, because something had to go into the abyss, took a can of beer from the refrigerator.

And thought uneasily a few minutes later, sauce for the gander. Lucy had at least gotten rid of her punch (although perhaps, all things considered, it might be regarded as a potion) but he had not, and now it stirred lazily. He did not want to start his companion off on any

92

lively discussion but could think of nothing calm and drowsy to say, with the result that Lucy stared bemusedly at him and he divided benign smiles between her and the rug while the silence settled over them like aspic. It occurred to him with an involuntary twitch of the mouth corners that it was too bad they had no materials for whittling.

Fortunately, the trancelike situation didn't last. Lucy suddenly snapped her eyelids wide, tossed her fair head, said with clarity and briskness, "I'm going to bed," and got to her feet, betrayed only by a sharp and immediate collision with the lamp table. She seemed to be headed for the couch. Justin, leaping up, steered her firmly into the bedroom, where she subsided obediently; took off her shoes, pulled the coverlet over her. Five minutes later, when her even breathing took no notice of his light pat on her shoulder, he closed the door of the darkened apartment behind him and went out to his car.

The snowfall was beginning to diminish; here, at any rate. To Justin, born and brought up in Connecticut, New Mexico weather seemed astonishingly localized: What was a mild rain in one spot might be rushing in the gutters three blocks away. There was an arroyo to cross on the way to Mrs. Balsam's, and although the gauge showed enough gas to get him there and back in spite of his unplanned detour past Amanda's house, it made no allowance for rocking and revving in the event of getting stuck.

Perhaps because of his sustained lack of food, or that somnolent little period of waiting for Lucy to go safely to sleep, his sense of immediacy was losing its edge. Besides, another explanation had presented itself. This would be Mrs. Balsam's first Christmas as a widow. What more likely than, to divert her mind from the fact, she had persuaded Amanda to go away with her over the holiday? She liked Santa Fe, and had a number of friends there.

This hypothesis did not take into account Mrs. Lopez's wild harangue on the telephone, but anybody who could plant fifty King Alfred daffodils upside down (according to Amanda) was not entirely to be trusted about plans or arrangements. Having paused in a coin-flipping way at the end of Lucy's driveway, Justin wiped the misted windshield with his palm and turned toward home.

Amanda, who had her tires checked regularly and had never driven on even one flat, wrestled grimly with the crippled car, the snow, her own nerves.

As soon as she was out of the driveway, she had fished one-handedly through the glove compartment and found an ancient cigarette so drained of tobacco at one end that it flared like a torch when she lit it. It tasted like engine grime and dead perfume, and she put it out almost at once because this was a job that required both hands and all her attention.

At a bare fifteen miles an hour, she might have been in command of an angry metal bull—or partial command, because the steering answered erratically while the framework bucked in its protestations. From the vibration, it seemed possible that something would break or fall off at any moment, or even that the car would pancake into the snow in a subsidence of nuts and bolts.

It should not have mattered at such a time that she hated what she was doing to the car. She had respected and taken scrupulous care of it, and she flinched from this deliberate abuse, no matter how necessary, in much the same way that she flinched from women who

94

dragged stumbling, crying children along pavements at a punishing adult pace.

Was there still slashed rubber flapping around, or was she now proceeding on pure wheels? Impossible to tell in the snow; equally impossible to know where the shoulder lay. Amanda drove in the middle of the road, bright lights blazing into whiteness that was now whirling as the wind came up, trying to remember whether the arroyo came before or after the abruptly quenched glimmer of lights that had indicated a house.

Because this clanking vehicle would never make it up a steepish slope.

She didn't have to worry about the arroyo. She hit something without warning, a rock or a pothole, and the wheel jerked sharply in her tense grip. She overcorrected, confused by the jolt and the spinning brilliance, and all at once the car was sharply canted, with two wheels in a ditch. Something—the rear axle?—had broken.

In her despair, Amanda struck the edge of the steering wheel savagely with a clenched fist. Rosie, who had been a core of rigidity because even at two she sensed something odd about this noisy faltering progress, now began to draw deep quivering breaths as significant, to anyone who knew her, as a pitcher's windup motion. Amanda said automatically, "Don't, Rosie," because the child's inclination toward sobs was dangerously tempting. The engine had stalled. She started it again, felt the right front and rear wheels churn uselessly, switched off the ignition.

What to do? She had alternately coaxed and forced the car almost a mile, because just ahead and on her right, not more than five yards back from the road, was the black shape of a small, long-deconsecrated church. Amanda had been in it once; it was narrow and low

95

ceilinged, with space for only eight or ten short pews on either side of the center aisle. Its windows were broken, and elm seedlings had started up in places where the plank flooring had crumbled.

Was there a very faint suggestion, below her and around a long curve, of car headlights?

She had fortified herself earlier by the possibility of encountering another motorist to whom she could signal distress by using her flashers and her horn. Now she realized that a driver on this approach almost had to be on his way to Mrs. Balsam's house.

At this hour, on his way back to Mrs. Balsam's house.

The tinge of pallor vanished, but Amanda felt as if she had been warned and would not be warned again. Her car had turned into a trap; the church at least would not be a tight little corner. There was the matter of footprints, but the wind and snow should smooth them over quite soon. If the man in the raincoat came upon the abandoned car he might easily think—because that decoying female voice would certainly have reported that she would try to find someone to catch the palomino—that a friend had indeed arrived and rescued her and Rosie, the tire tracks buried by snow.

It was fear and not logic which put forward the idea of a return at all. Logic said that that descent upon the house in spite of the failed bid to lure her out of it argued a plan which had to be implemented without delay; that the man who called himself Peter Dickens had delivered that faceless entity from the cellar somewhere and was busily piling up miles in a different direction.

Fear had no rationalization, and needed none. Ridiculously, as if the exact location of footprints mattered, Amanda wriggled over the gear shift so that she could get out of the car on the passenger side. She plucked up

Rosie in her blanket, locked that door too, and ran under a partly collapsed adobe archway, snow spilling into her shoes. The church door opened readily under her hand.

Tiny by day, it was cavernous by match light. No altar remained, or stand for votive candles, although there were vestiges of tile which had been Stations of the Cross. There was a single tipped-over pew which, righted, would make a temporary bed for Rosie. From somewhere, in the smell of cold and decayed wood, came an inquisitive rustle. Nesting birds? Rats?

Amanda's current match went out and she lit another, instinctively, in this place, pinching them out and dropping them into her pocket. She said to the restively stirring Rosie, "We'll sit down in a minute," but she should not have spoken; her own voice, deadened and diminished in this forgotten air, frightened her.

Up front and to the right there was a confessional. Amanda approached it, to investigate for purposes of concealment, and opened the nearest door. It seemed to take forever for Ellie Peale to come toppling stiffly out.

Chapter 10

By macabre chance, the dead face had assumed the exact angle of the photograph used to saturation point in newspapers and on the television screen, so that it took no buried foreknowledge to recognize this particular contour of white cheek, this feathery brown hair. The dark eyes were open but unfathomable: Ellie Peale had recorded no impression of the eternity into which she had been prematurely thrust. There wasn't a great deal of blood on the front of the cream shirt. The knife must have—

Amanda dropped the match away and backed away, trembling. In the midst of her horror and pity there was a frightful sense of intimacy, as though Ellie Peale, now serene, were charting the way for her. In the natural course of events her casual resting place would have been, for the winter months at least, as secret as any under grass; with its bell removed and its little tower fallen the church was not of the kind to attract wandering tourists—and how many peeked into confessionals in any case?

Stuffed there, like an awkward parcel. "Bless me, Father, for I have been murdered."

Rosie had not shared in that flickering glimpse of death, because when she struggled higher in her blanketed perch on Amanda's hip and suggested anxiously, "We go home?" it was only with a restless dislike of this strange dark place.

"Yes, in a minute," said Amanda, collecting herself with an enormous effort. They would have to get out of here, although home was an impossible sound that made her throat swell. It was not only unthinkable to stay, it could be mortally dangerous. Take boldly to the road in the remembered direction of house lights? Or, if the church had a side door, flounder across fields—provided that they weren't fenced—even though it meant exposing Rosie to the cold for longer?

Shock at that terrible thumping emergence from the confessional had rendered her dizzied, incapacitated, despairingly certain that whatever decision she made would be the wrong one. Her wet feet were icy, her cradling arm and shoulder ached even though Rosie, clinging to her with spindly arms and legs, supported most of her own weight.

Amanda did not light another match, in case its brief glow might reach out and appear to make Ellie Peale twitch wistfully. Her sharp retreat had brought her halfway to the toppled pew. She proceeded cautiously, tipped it upright, and put the child down for a few moments of physical relief, flexing her arm and saying in a whisper, "Don't move, Rosie, I'll be right back."

The priest traditionally entered from the left, so that if there were a side door it would be there. Amanda touched the frigid wall and trailed her fingertips guidingly along it for perhaps five steps before she checked. A vehicle with a quiet engine, the kind which had purred away from Mrs. Balsam's house, was nearing the church.

Let it go by, she prayed wildly, but it did not. The soft steady hum came to a pause—while the snow was inspected for footprints?—and died. A car door slammed, with either a carrying echo or the almost-synchronized sound of a second one.

Even if she had already located the side exit there wouldn't be time to go back for Rosie and retrace her steps. Amanda caught a breath that missed being a sob by only a hair, found the pew again, got down with the child on the rough plank floor. The pew had legs at such intervals that it was impossible to slide under it. Rosie, startled and alarmed at this summary treatment, began a protest which Amanda cut off with a peremptory "Ssh!" She prepared herself to put a stifling palm over the small mouth if necessary, and the church door opened.

There were obviously two of them, as silent and purposeful as commandos. They had a flashlight, a strong one, more stabbing white than yellow. Amanda, squeezing her eyes childishly shut, knew exactly when the brilliant probe struck the open door of the confessional and then the body of Ellie Peale. The two pairs of feet halted and then proceeded; there was an indistinguishable mutter—sickened, she imagined it to be something like, "You take her legs"—and then some fast bundling and bumping, culminating in a woody thud.

Almost without transition, because this was the only other place in the church offering even elementary cover, she was pinned in light, and Peter Dickens said, "Here she is."

*   *   *

101

It might have been some ugly game. Amanda got to her feet, made awkward by failure and humiliation more than by her burden. She said steadily into the blinding flare, "I don't know who you are, either of you, but if I don't return this child to her parents right away, and they can't reach me, they'll call the police."

No pause at all; they had expected this. "You'll have to call the parents then, won't you?" said Dickens. His voice was mockingly reasonable. "Come on, let's go."

Neither man touched her as she walked up the aisle in the directed flashlight beam, but she felt as if there were a cattle prod or something far worse poised just behind her shoulder. With echoes no longer mattering, she said clearly to the stilled and shrinking child, "Don't worry, I'm going to call your father and we'll have you home in just a few minutes. He's a deputy sheriff, by the way," she lied as a bold afterthought.

Rosie understood "your father" because Amanda had always found something arch about "your daddy"—but at once, in order to remind her that there was no safe harbor, she said fearfully, "Daddy all go—"

"Because he'll be worried," said Amanda, rushing to cover that and feeling obscurely that as long as she was talking she had some measure of control over her situation, "and so will your mother."

"Daddy all gone, huh?" observed Dickens alertly, and then they were out in the windy cold.

It was still snowing. Amanda glanced automatically at her own earlier footprints, now shallow depressions visible only to someone looking for them. If she had had ten minutes more? But they would still have looked inside the church, knowing what it held, and even if she had had the courage and the strength to return Ellie Peale to concealment they would have followed the traces of moisture from her wet shoes and tracked her down like an animal.

Without a word, she was shepherded—Dickens in front, Ellie Peale's still-unseen killer behind—toward a green pickup. It was like a stone in her chest to remember Maria Lopez, glowing in her cream pantsuit and blue eye makeup, handing over her fragile child and saying, "I can't thank you enough. Merry Christmas. . . ."

At least, thought Amanda numbly as Dickens opened the door with an imperative gesture, it was not the murder van.

The van had been stolen, as confidently expected by Sweet, half an hour after he had abandoned it near Contessa Park two nights earlier.

Leaving a vehicle untended in this area, even without the keys in the ignition, was tantamount to leaving a roast of beef accessible in a house which contained a dog. Contessa Park, handy to a number of bars which tailed into the local skid row, was a magnet for petty criminals, vagrants, groups of malcontents, troublemakers of every variety. It was not unusual for a band of youths to while away a summer afternoon attacking any innocents who strayed into the park to shoot baskets on a cracked cement apron, and passing cars occasionally had their windshields shattered. Unless specifically summoned, the police inclined to give the place a wide berth.

A number of people came to New Mexico for reasons of health. So, indirectly, had Sal Arcudi, for whom there were eight warrants out in his native California. He had annexed to himself en route a stray named Shirley, a fact which mystified all who saw her: At nineteen she had a figure which seemed heavily and unsuccessfully corseted, and a countenance so forbidding that it suggested knitting and a scaffold.

Sal was down to his last twenty dollars, and Shirley to her last seven and her mother's watch, when they came upon the van, keys in place. It could not have been called a jewel—its seats were splitting and only bright slivers remained of its rearview mirror—but there was half a tank of gas and Sal knew of a thicket along the river where they could pull in and, for a time, subsist. They were off in a twinkling.

Not surprisingly, because the police bulletin had been late in its issuance and there was no year, make, or even exact color to go by, they reached their destination unmolested. Both Sal and Shirley slept late in the morning, bundled into the sleeping bags they had traveled with, and when Shirley finally trudged up to the road and found a store where she could buy sweet rolls and a can of fruit juice, the morning papers had long since been sold out.

The van's radio did not work until Sal, bored, skilled with his fingers, brought it to life by early afternoon. They listened to the news, in search of the weather forecast because they were contemplating El Paso, and stared at each other in wild surmise. There was no blood in the van, as far as they could see, but they might very well be stopped routinely on a highway. In addition to being wanted in California, Sal was five feet eleven and dark haired, and his fingerprints were now all over the van.

They wiped the surfaces with thoroughness, only realizing when they had finished that *if* this were the vehicle used in the abduction—and here they remembered those inviting keys—they might have erased the prints that mattered and inadvertently left one of Sal's somewhere.

104

It was imperative to put distance between themselves and the van. The autumn winds had brought down a lot of small debris, and they piled it over the roof and hood, cementing it with matted cottonwood leaves; Shirley, growing tired and mulish, nevertheless made a number of trips up to the road to report on the effect. Then they took measuring stock of each other.

Shirley's face was square; she wore her dark-blonde hair in grimly coroneted braids; even at a glance she weighed a good thirty pounds more than the missing girl described on the radio. Sal had begun to sprout a Fu Manchu moustache, but it was still wispy enough to go unnoticed at a distance and in spite of the need for haste he took time to darken it generously with Shirley's eyebrow pencil. Together, sleeping bags rolled and lashed to their backs, they would pass easily as a pair of sociology majors getting a late start home for the Christmas holidays.

Speed notwithstanding, they had done well. When they gained the road and glanced back and down, the van was invisible to any but an educated eye.

It was some time before Amanda realized that the pickup's radio was turned to the police band. What was being said in a monotonous male voice with frequent crackling pauses in between was unintelligible to her, but she supposed that it would alert criminals to the progress of the opposition.

She sat rigidly in the middle, patting the child on her lap now and then as she might have patted a trembling puppy, trying to flinch her shoulders inward from any contact with Dickens, at the wheel, or the silent shape on her other side. She had glanced at him elliptically once, under the pretext of rearranging strayed folds of Rosie's blanket. His profile was set and queerly blunted,

105

and although he was utterly motionless he gave an impression of being ready to spring. He must have been wearing a dark wig when he took Ellie Peale from the convenience store, because the dim light from the dashboard picked out a smooth edge of blondish hair.

Eeriness being the very fabric of nightmare, it did not seem odd to Amanda that what she had seen in the church, and what they had bundled back into the confessional, was not mentioned in that short and purposeful drive through the snow. She would not have dared, sandwiched in between the killer and his accessory, and they scarcely needed to bring her situation home to her.

The radio muttered. Rosie, lulled by sound and motion, normally oblivious in her crib by six o'clock, had fallen asleep. Amanda held herself so tense in avoidance of the flanking men that her shoulders and the small of her back ached, and began to record with bared nerves the fact that the uncommunicativeness in the truck was more than lack of utterance. It had an explosive quality which she had encountered, watered down a number of times, upon entering a room where there had just been a fierce domestic quarrel. Were they at odds as to what to do about her, the witness? Or was it simply concerted rage over a miscarriage in their plans?

Here was the lighted crossroads and the telephone booth, snow topped, its glass wooled over. Dickens backed the pickup into darkness, pulled on the brake but left the motor running, reached into the glove compartment for the flashlight. He opened the door and got out. "Come on, make your call," he said, and then, when Amanda maneuvered across the seat with Rosie balanced against her shoulder, "The kid stays."

With the man who had plunged a knife into Ellie

Peale? "I won't leave her," said Amanda, trying for calm. "You can't make—"

"You don't think so?" He didn't bother to be sardonic; he was brief and matter-of-fact. "She'll be okay if you do as you're told."

And there was the pattern, stark and unbreakable. As long as one of them had Rosie, and a vehicle in which to drive off with her to some unfindable place, she would indeed do as she was told. With a swarm of hatred that burned just under her ribs, Amanda set the sleepily stirring child down on the seat, said gently, "I'll be right back," and, because there were times which demanded the deliberate self-infliction of pain, jumped savagely out into the snow.

Her ankle, stiffened and swollen, responded with a searing flash that made her catch her breath. Dickens did not comment on her limp as they walked to the telephone booth. Instead, he asked intently, "What happened to your aunt?"

Amanda was tempted fleetingly to say that thanks to him Mrs. Balsam had been very nearly frightened to death—but that would imply that she had recognized the man in her house as the subject of a police-artist's sketch. Certainly, given a description, she would be able to put a name to Dickens. He must not be allowed to think himself endangered in that way, with Ellie Peale's body revealed in the church, because then he would be forced—

"Nobody knows, except that it's her heart," said Amanda, sending up an apology because lies of this nature made her very uneasy. "They don't expect her to regain consciousness."

With her clear memory of the hospital room she did not have to pretend bleakness, and something about Dickens' alert glance at her suggested a small easing of

107

tension. He opened the door of the telephone booth, handed her two dimes, squeezed himself in with her. He said, "Tell them the snow is bad up here and the kid's asleep so you're staying the night," adding conversationally, "If you try anything, I blink the flashlight and he takes off."

How likely was he to let her near a telephone again, even standing so vigilantly close? Heart beating hard, Amanda dropped the coins in, dialed the Lopez number in her time-buying ploy, let it drawl ten times. "I can't understand it," she said. "They're never out this late. Maybe the snow . . . I suppose they could have had an accident, but the first thing they'll do is try to reach—"

"They must have neighbors, or friends you can leave a message with," said Dickens. His pleasant voice had acquired a grate. "Don't tell me—"

"Well, there's his brother," said Amanda carefully, stomach tightening. "They don't get along, but I suppose he'd leave a note on their door."

At Dickens' curt order she lifted the chained telephone directory, opened it to the L's, pretended to seek out one particular Lopez from a double-page spread of them. The type shifted and blurred in front of her eyes. Justin would know her voice no matter how she addressed him, would realize that she was speaking under duress, would—what?

Amanda couldn't imagine, but neither could she walk away from her one chance at communication having made no effort at all. She retrieved the two dimes, dropped them in, and dialed.

Chapter 11

Oblique distress signals tumbled through her head as she listened to the ringing commence at the other end; she refused to entertain the possibility that it was echoing once more through an empty apartment.

"The snow's fairly deep up here and I've never really learned to drive in it." It was New England–bred Justin who had taught her how to reduce the possibility of skids to a minimum.

And: "Tell Maria not to bother phoning me—" Dickens ought to approve of this "—because everything's fine and I'm just going to bed myself." In her agitation over Amanda's nonappearance Maria must have gotten it across that they were depending upon her because of their arranged flight east.

What gave her away? A very slight tremor of the tightly gripped receiver as she realized the risk she was running in this total dependence on Justin's quick-wittedness? From behind, Dickens suddenly reached around and wrenched the receiver from her hand. Amanda saw the silhouetted flashlight, his thumb ready on the button, poised against the snow outside and aimed in the direction of the waiting pickup. He said, fast and dangerous, "What's your name?"

"Amanda. Morley." She had to add it, to defuse these perilous few seconds.

A further burr, and then Justin: "Hello?" Amanda closed her eyes; it seemed the final bitterness, after her vain attempts to reach him from Mrs. Balsam's house, that she could hear him quite clearly. He sounded eager and out of breath, as though he had battled with his door key to answer this summons.

"Mr. Lopez?"

Justin, going flat: "I'm afraid you have the wrong—"

"Oh, wait, sorry, that's someone I've been trying to reach for the last five minutes." Which could happen easily; Amanda had often made this kind of mistake. "I'm calling for Amanda, there seems to be trouble on that line. She's at Mrs. Balsam's, taking care of Apple and the horse while her aunt's away and baby-sitting at the same time. We had quite a job getting Rosie to sleep —strange house, I guess—and she wanted me to let you know that she's staying there tonight."

We. The intimacy of putting a small child to bed, possibly taking turns with stories, probably having a drink afterward by way of mutual congratulation. Was Justin believing it? There was no reason why he shouldn't. He didn't know about her self-imposed solitary evenings, and Dickens was projecting himself as courteous and civilized; no one listening to him would dream of a snatched receiver, a menacing flashlight. Mrs. Balsam, not naive, had trusted him to the extent that he had access to her house and the cellar into which he had introduced a killer.

110

The unsuspected cellar, which held a special bafflement: It had no windows, and surely that was unusual?

" . . . I see. I tried the house and couldn't get an answer," said Justin, now neutral, and Amanda, hearing that, imagining the welcome ring and the familiar voice, clenched her hands hopelessly. Where had she been? Out feeding the palomino? Wrestling the car along the road? Or—hardest of all to bear—standing frozen in Mrs. Balsam's bedroom, listening to the telephone ring and whispering to Rosie that they wouldn't answer it?

She could turn her head right now and cry, "Help!" and no matter how fast Dickens was Justin would hear. But by the time he had called the police (with no idea of where this call was originating) and they had taken his name and address, and hers and very possibly Rosie's, and inquired as to his place in all this, what would have happened to her, and where would Rosie be?

Justin was saying something about the storm, and then: "Thanks for calling, Mr. . . . ?" He was careful about such details, and of course he would think he was getting a real name.

"Williams." Let him try looking that up, in case some oddity occurred to him and he wanted to call back. "No trouble. Goodnight." Dickens was friendly and brisk—until he hung up the receiver, opened the door for a shower of weak gold light, turned on Amanda. If there had been more room in the booth, she knew that he would have swung the flashlight at her face. The openness that he could will into his eyes had been replaced by a cold and blazing rage. "Goddamn you, I ought—"

He stared out at the pickup, visibly controlling himself, and then back at Amanda, lashes narrowing as he

111

added up the hour, the snow, the fact of a semi-invalid child. "The parents aren't expecting her back tonight, are they?"

Amanda, briefly unable to speak, shook her head.

"Understand one thing. That kid is nothing to me, *nothing.* She doesn't look like she's got too long anyway," said Dickens with casual brutality. "Another trick out of you and she's going to get mislaid someplace. Have you got that?"

Amanda nodded mutely and then, sensing a return of his fury, said, "Yes. All right."

Her whole being echoed with shock as she walked ahead of him back to the pickup. She had thought she recognized Dickens for what he was, a man without scruple of any kind, trading on his looks as successfully as an attractive and poisonous plant, but insensibly, because outward appearance had a tendency to govern even in the face of facts, she had relied upon his being the more rational of the two, the more approachable. She had been wrong. He might be better balanced than the man who had walked into a store and carried a girl off to her death, but he was nakedly singleminded: He was going to get them both out of this at whatever cost, and his commitment made his temper a terrifying thing.

From her exhausted little sniffles and gasps, Rosie had been crying. Had she simply run out of energy, or had she been stopped with a slap? In the pickup, Amanda gathered her close and kissed a wet cheek, trying to communicate comfort with her arms. *That kid is nothing to me, nothing.*

Someone braver might have asked boldly as the truck was set in motion, "Where are you taking us? What are you going to do with us?" To Amanda, who had never deceived herself about being brave when it came to

112

physical threat, any questions seemed better unasked. In a silence—could the man on her right conceivably be a mute?—broken only by the staccato and incomprehensible mutterings from the radio, they turned in the direction of Mrs. Balsam's house.

To lock her and Rosie in the cellar?

At the very thought, Amanda's toes curled in her icy shoes. She had never been in a cellar—most Southwestern houses were not so equipped, being built directly on slab—but in fiction at least they were places of rodents, cobwebs, impromptu burials. This one, windowless, would be utterly black. She tried to reassure herself by the fact that Dickens had been forced to mention Mrs. Balsam's house to Justin—but how much risk was that, with his easy use of her name, and Rosie's and the Afghan's? Justin would imagine them all bedded down for the night, warm and safe.

And there was no one else.

They passed the church with its hidden, unstirring occupant—and then her car, looking almost prehistorically dead in its snowy shroud. With the drifting and powdering of white, no one could guess at the state of its tires.

The pickup jolted sharply as one wheel struck whatever it was that Amanda had hit earlier. The hitherto voiceless man let out a harsh strangled protest, and Dickens swung his head to glance across at him. "Okay, hang on, we'll get you something."

That peculiar rigidity, with its suggestion of crouch: Was he a drug addict; had he killed Ellie Peale in some disoriented frenzy? Or—for the first time Amanda remembered the two ransacked medicine cabinets—was it possible that she had managed to harm him before she died, featherweight though she was?

113

With startling suddenness the headlights reached out to a familiar stretch of rail fence, the quenched black glimmer of windows, a snowed-over dark blue Volkswagen Rabbit. For the second time that night, Amanda had arrived at Mrs. Balsam's house.

In the instant before Dickens cut the ignition, she had a feeling of total unreality. It seemed incredible, in her present circumstances, that she had ever come here with the simple notion of feeding the dog and the horse; that, even entrusted with the forgotten Rosie, she had cooked her dinner, watched the televised news, said goodnight without a qualm to tall, erect Colonel Robinson while all this was gathering around her. (But there had been a moment of real fear before she found the light switch inside the front door; had the very air carried a warning?)

Apple was letting off a volley of deep-throated barks. "Out," said Dickens tersely, holding the door open on his side and jerking his head at Rosie. "Leave her here."

"I can't. She has to go to the bathroom," said Amanda, equally curt, and it was true that Rosie had begun some anxious fidgeting. "She's only two."

" . . . Okay," said Dickens with obvious distaste. He leaned past Amanda as she got out, addressing the other man. "Come on."

As a safeguard, in case she could put her hand on a weapon in the house? Of course she could; any kitchen was full of them. The drawer where she had found the flashlight for her expedition to the corral also had contained skewers, a roasting fork, all-purpose scissors. Useless, even if they would allow her into the kitchen, with a child as pawn.

At the front door, Dickens produced a ring of keys which Amanda supposed were a duplicate of her aunt's, found the right one without difficulty, did not have to

114

feel for the light switch. This casual almost-ownership was a ridiculous thing to register a tiny flare of rage at, and it certainly didn't matter that one off-white wall now wore a jagged splash of yellow-brown or that a smashed mustard bottle had leaked the rest of its contents onto the gray-blue rug.

After her first horror at having to sort out three people the Afghan came forward in a hostessy rush, dancing first to Amanda and then to Dickens, keeping well away from his companion. The bulbs on the miniature Christmas tree caught a current of air and made curtsies in rose and pink and silver. Amanda turned her head and gazed inescapably at the man who had risen nightmarishly out of the floor.

Inevitably, because the black girl's glimpse of him in the convenience store had been alarmed and fleeting, he bore only a passing resemblance to the artist's sketch. There was a certain flattening to the opaque-skinned features, but his mouth was almost arrogantly defined, his face pointed rather than oval. He wore jeans and a denim jacket. His long dark eyes stared back at her as intensely as a strange animal's.

He held his right hand, the clear cause of his concentrated stillness, curved stiffly in front of him, elbow out as though supported by an invisible sling. The flesh was swollen and inflamed and glazed-looking, suggesting a red-hot throb which would have made Amanda wince if it had been anyone else. Had Ellie Peale used her teeth in her desperation, or had he encountered a scorpion or black widow in the cellar?

"Come on, make it snappy," said Dickens edgily, and Amanda removed her magnetized glance and followed him along the hall, accompanied by Apple. He entered Mrs. Balsam's bathroom ahead of her, made a swift inspection of the medicine cabinet, took out and pock-

115

eted the safety razor and packet of blades. His frightening gloves—from a surgical supply store?—fitted him as tightly and shinily as healed burns.

An icy little breath was seeping from behind the locked door of Mrs. Balsam's bedroom, where the window stood wide, but Dickens' attention was elsewhere as he stepped back to let Amanda pass. "Hurry up," he said. "And fix your face."

Fix her . . . ? Amanda could scarcely believe she had heard that. He was nervous, she thought, perching Rosie; he had been forced out of his usual poise, and he wasn't used to it. It was not a cause for elation. Perhaps out of that enforced physical closeness in the phone booth, she was beginning to develop what was almost a rapport with Dickens, and something told her that there was a new core of fury in him which might erupt all over her as surrogate.

And she knew now why they were all here.

It was some time since she had seen Rosie in the light, and a fresh worry assailed her as she washed the small face and hands, rapidly, because she did not want to be ordered out of here. The child's huge dark eyes seemed to have retreated, her always peaked features looked wizened. Rosie, who had survived in a cocoon of protection—

Her forehead didn't feel hot. Still, Amanda reached into the cabinet for two aspirins to drop into her pocket, in case of emergency, and was confronted by her own reflection.

Her top-piled hair had continued to escape fringily. Only a ghost of her lipstick remained. Heavy dust picked up in the church had somehow become transferred to her face, emphasizing her pallor and the eyes which were at present her only real color; she might have been an evacuee from some natural disaster, and

116

that did not fit in with Dickens' plan.

Too bad, thought Amanda, and realized on the heels of that that there were two of them, that Dickens might just be vengeful enough to spit on his handkerchief and — She used soap and water, toweled her face dry, said urgently to Rosie, "They aren't going to hurt us, but don't cry, they don't like it," and opened the door. She was just in time: Dickens was starting along the hall, his face set.

"I have to get Rosie's pills," said Amanda quickly. "They're in the guest room."

Because he would have only contemptuous dismissal for vitamins, and how long before (don't look at any other possibility) would they be released and safe? As it was, another echo of distaste came from Dickens, but after a second's hesitation he walked to the guest room door, again entering first.

Amanda went at once to the small suitcase. With a businesslike economy that made her heart sink, Dickens straightened the scarcely disturbed covers on the near twin bed, erasing the fact that Rosie had slept there. The Afghan had bustled in, convinced that she was a member of a happy group, and Amanda cast a glance of despair at the delicate golden face that came dipping inquisitively into the suitcase. Apple was a fast and wiry jumper. If she had been of another breed, the kind ready to attack on command—but she was not. Having discovered that there was nothing edible among Rosie's scanty belongings, she was nosing affectionately at Dickens' hand.

It wasn't only affection, Amanda realized, dropping the bottle of vitamins into her coat pocket as she stood up; it was expectation as well. Apple was looking to Dickens for her dinner because at some previous time he had fed her. He was of course—it fell neatly into

117

place, very late—the man who had returned her to Mrs. Balsam and refused a reward.

And hadn't there been something about repairs to the corral, so that he would know the quickest and easiest point at which to let the mare out? Wonderment at the delay in her own recognition brought Amanda's gaze up from the dog to Dickens' eyes, blue, a little narrowed, watching and aware.

But he considered Mrs. Balsam as good as dead. It would certainly not cross his mind to telephone the hospital and perhaps learn—

Apple backed precipitately into her shins. "Your— that man seems to have an infected hand," said Amanda, pretending not to have caught motion in the hall behind Dickens. "I have streptomycin and codeine at home."

She did, as legacy of a severe attack of tonsillitis. Like the feigned necessity for calling the Lopezes, it was a desperate time-gaining maneuver, a delay in Dickens' plan for her—and the man in the doorway, speaking for the first time, said abruptly, "Then let's go there."

His voice was heavy and soft and edgeless, like condensed fog. Dickens looked hard at Amanda and walked out of the guest room. From the far end of the hall there was some urgent muttering and then the unmistakable impact of a fist smashing against the wall, a statement of rage and pain.

Dickens came back, his face tight. "I warned you once, but I'll warn you again." His icy stare shifted to Rosie and stayed there for a deliberate heartbeat or two. "If you don't have that stuff, all hell is going to break loose."

It did not need embroidering. "I have it," said Amanda.

In the living room, she had a long tense moment

118

alone with the other man, who paced without speaking in a kind of lithe shamble, before the other part of the house went dark and Dickens appeared with her hand-bag and the keys to the Rabbit. Mrs. Balsam's bag, from which he had taken them, was nowhere to be seen—was he afraid that a cleaning woman might come in the morning and wonder why her employer had gone off without it?

Apple had given up on Dickens, now glancing around him and moving purposefully in the direction of the front door, and raised a fringy paw to scrape remindingly at Amanda's coat. The dog was unaware of any perfidy, and her eyes glowed with trust. She had been all day without food, and Amanda remembered the water bowl in the kitchen as being empty too. "Can't I at least feed—?"

"No," said Dickens, a short chop of sound, and once again, as she had known he must, took Rosie from her and nodded at the denim-clad man. "He rides with you."

Rosie did not struggle over the transfer; unaware of impending separation, she simply turned her small questioning face to Amanda, whose throat closed before it would allow her to say steadily, "We're going for a ride, Rosie. We're going to my house."

Dickens had a finger on the light switch. He did not ask directions, as if that would allow Amanda to lead him on a wild-goose chase or even to the house of the man to whom she had tried to send a distress signal. He said only, "I'll be behind you, all the way. Better be careful not to lose me."

He plunged the living room into darkness then, and Amanda walked out into the night ahead of both men, hearing Apple's disappointed whimpers as the door closed with finality. The Volkswagen's windows had to

119

be cleared of snow, and that was left to her, but in less than two minutes she was in the driver's seat, hands wet and burning with cold because at some unrememberable point she had lost her gloves, with Ellie Peale's murderer beside her.

When he had said goodnight to Amanda's friend Williams, Justin proceeded to his kitchen to make himself the most delicious meal that occurred to him in his extremity: a fried egg sandwich. He felt as if he had not eaten in two days.

He had been half right in his latest surmise, he reflected, disinterring a small iron pan with the resultant shrieking collapse of every other cooking vessel he owned; Mrs. Balsam was away. It was reassuring to know that Amanda was safely under cover, in this weather, but there was something undeniably flat about receiving the information secondhand. To an ear in the inveterate habit of attaching flesh and blood to disembodied voices, Williams had sounded tall, correct, and well dressed. (But would he have expected Amanda to take up with a rude threadbare dwarf?)

Butter to sizzle; presently, egg. A familiar feeling was beginning to steal over Justin, but he ignored it and pressed two slices of bread down into the toaster; white, which he bought occasionally under the censorious regard of shoppers with brown or black loaves. Amanda was also of the whole-wheat persuasion, although where liver pâté and transparent rings of onion were concerned her principles fell by the wayside.

Amanda. For just a second she seemed to look at him out of the air: copper-brown hair which she wore in a variety of ways, very clear and noticing greenish eyes, long vertical dimple in her right cheek when she smiled. It was warming but odd that she had thought to relay a message to him on the evening when he had discovered her to be an absolute necessity, but hadn't been able to tell her so or find out whether she felt even remotely the same way about him.

He assembled his sandwich, distributing a little ketchup here and there along with salt and pepper. And the inevitable happened: Ravenous hunger had turned into the full and leaden feeling of having eaten far too much. He took a single bite, had to chew interminably to force it down his throat, deposited his handiwork in the garbage, and went morosely to bed.

Chapter 12

I'll be behind you, all the way.

Amanda had never driven the Rabbit, and would have felt a certain hesitance with a strange dashboard and a different response even by herself on a dry sunlit road. Under Dickens' stark threat, her hands had a tendency to shake, and after she had located the windshield-wiper knob she got into reverse with a noise that suggested gear-stripping, wobbled her way into first, skidded going out of the driveway because the accelerator pedal was a livelier one than her own. The pickup's headlights began to follow steadily.

Which of them had the knife used to slash her tires? It could not be the murder weapon, because no sane man . . . and there went that argument.

She had known when she saw the grotesque hand of the man beside her that she was to be recruited as driver in an enforced change of plan. Had they found their bolthole closed, or been alerted by something on the police radio? Whichever the case, there was an element of safety in this particular dividing. The authorities by now might be thinking in terms of a body rather than a captive, but would they be looking for Ellie Peale's killer in the company of a woman?

Amanda, glancing up at the headlights in the rearview mirror, discovered that she did not even want to think about the police at the moment. Would she dare, in the unlikely event of meeting a patrol car, slew deliberately toward it and stake everything on one fast burst: "This is the man who murdered Ellie Peale and the truck behind me has a kidnapped child in it"?

No, she would not. No officer would act instantly on such a wild declaration—she could envision being asked for her driver's license and registration—and she believed implicitly Dickens' statement that he would mislay Rosie if he felt threatened. He was hanging well back, and once they were off this stretch of road he would be able to dart off into the night if he chose. And, approaching it from the front, she had never seen the pickup's license plate.

. . . Here was the crossroads, and the telephone booth where she had listened helplessly to Justin's acceptance of her and Rosie's safety and well-being. If she had known then that the man in the passenger seat was incapable of driving away at a signal from the flashlight . . . ? Even now, with the memory of that savage impact of fist against wall, she would not have risked it.

Ahead and below were the scattered streetlights of the town center, a quarter-mile of small businesses, bars and eating places, tiny library, police and fire stations. Having grown somewhat more accustomed to the car, Amanda reached for the pack of Mrs. Balsam's cigarettes on the dashboard, shook one free, lit it with a match from the accompanying folder. At once, the

124

man who had been staring silently out the side window swung his head and said in his strange voice, "Put that out. I'm allergic."

Allergic. Having stopped a young girl's heart with a knife, and so recently helped cram her body back into hiding, he was troubled by secondhand smoke. Accumulated hatred and rage boiled up into Amanda's throat. "What a shame. Open the window," she said, and defiantly lifted her cigarette again.

Instantly, it was snatched from her with such force that its core struck the inside of the steering wheel, scattering bright fragments into her lap. A smell of burning wool arose. After one lightning glance downward she kept her eyes on the road while she slapped at her coat, but the car had taken a sharp little veer.

"Watch it," said the man conversationally with a backward jerk of his head. "He doesn't like that kid."

Amanda didn't answer him. She had drawn a deep trembling breath and was saying calmingly to herself that smoking (like ingesting certain food dyes and nitrites and saccharine, and being exposed to asphalt and standing at curbside in big-city rush-hour traffic and drinking the water in some places) was not really a good idea, and that from cutting down she intended to stop completely.

But under the personal governance of this near-animal?

The traffic light at which she would turn left in the direction of her house blinked from yellow to red. The center might have looked festive an hour ago, but its Christmas decorations had been thriftily turned off, except for a little tree in a hardware store window, and its overhead ropes of tinsel and stars were extinguished by the snow. The town was not quite asleep, however; on the near corner, the door of Shelley's Bar and Grille started open and then fell shut, as though someone inside were saying protracted goodnights.

These men need me, at least right now, realized Amanda suddenly, and not with a noticeably black eye or a cut lip. As the door of the bar opened and a man and woman emerged, she reached for the cigarettes and matches. "I'm driving you because I have to, but that's all," she said steadily. "I didn't have to tell you that I have medicine for your hand, and I am going to smoke this cigarette."

The match flame shook, but that might have been attributed to a window not quite closed. The couple from the bar crossed the street in front of them, heads turning automatically, providing a measure of insulation in an electric moment. Amanda drew in smoke, flicked on her turn signal, and put the car gently in motion as the light changed. She didn't really want the cigarette—indeed, it was making her heart beat very fast—but it had been for her an essential gesture, a brief handhold in this precipitous night, and she took another unhurried inhalation, when she had rounded the corner, before she tossed it out into the snow.

The man beside her was silent and unstirring. Had that earlier command been simply an exercise of power, to underline her subservient status?

The pickup now began to close the distance; in his ruffling through her handbag Dickens had obviously acquainted himself with her address. The last mile was almost totally dark, with luminarias extinguished until tomorrow night, although here and there a single window glowed and, three houses from Amanda's, a recessed porch was dressed up in strings of mortuary blue. With a sense of time running out, she pulled into her driveway.

But although her headlights had reflected off black

windows and the immediate neighborhood was clearly fast asleep, they were taking no chances. Instead of following her in, the pickup coasted to a stop at the mouth of the drive, ready to take off like a flash at any indication of a trap. Her abortive attempt to reach Justin, Amanda supposed; for all they knew, the "Morley" lettered in black on the mailbox might be her father or her brother.

She opened the door on her side before she could be ordered to and was dipping automatically into her bag when her passenger dangled her house keys between thumb and forefinger and then reached awkwardly across himself to manage his own door release. In view of what they had done and were doing, this casual appropriation of her property had a gnatlike insignificance; still, Amanda was stiff with anger as she marched ahead of him through the snow, scarcely feeling the pain in her ankle, and waited for admission to her house.

Had they thought there was a possibility that she would throw Rosie to the winds, manage to get into the house first, lock the door and call the police?

For that matter—this man would certainly want to make sure that the house was untenanted, and her telephone, on a corner table in the living room, had a soundless touch dial—was there a chance . . . ?

He gave her the keys to spare himself any left-handed fumbling, shouldered past her with a sudden fierce grip on her wrist, stood warily testing the warm dark silence before he swept the inner wall with his palm and encountered the light switch.

Amanda blinked at her little hall, as strange to her as if she had been away for a week. Its cream wallpaper had pencil stripes of grape and slate, the coatrack was occupied only by a raincoat and a blue-and-green Irish wool scarf, the carved chest held the morning's mail which she had dropped there unopened to answer her telephone and learn about Mrs. Balsam.

The living room to the left, light catching a quiver of silver from the Christmas tree in its depths, was the short end of the L which held kitchen, dining room which was scarcely more than a windowed alcove, tiny guest room, bedroom, and bath. The absolute stillness everywhere seemed to Amanda as proclamatory as a blank sheet of paper, but if she had even eight or nine seconds alone . . .

She tried, saying in a voice which invited echoes, "There's no one else here, I live by myself."

This drew a glance of near-contempt from the tense man at her side. In the unspeaking way which was beginning to get badly on her nerves—had he been like this with Ellie Peale?—he snapped the outside light on and off, signalingly. No wonder neither of the witnesses had been able to identify him as Anglo or Spanish, thought Amanda over tightened nerves; his opaque features and the length of his eyes looked, if anything, faintly Indian. Not American Indian, but the kind who ate missionaries on steamy riverbanks.

The pickup came quietly into the drive, and then Dickens walked in with Rosie.

Even before he set her down so jarringly that her spindly bow legs went out from under her, it was clear that the child had sparked off his temper by wailing out of fright and what must be a sense of total abandonment: One side of her tear-streaked face was a furious red. Far more alarmingly, she sat on the floor with the inertness of a potted plant, past protest, past belief in promises that no one was going to hurt her.

Amanda's heart shook. People said reassuringly in

128

times of crisis, "Children are tough," and while they might be right most of the time, Rosie wasn't tough. It seemed a fresh part of madness that she was here in this depleted state because the doctor had vetoed the plane trip east as too taxing.

"Go get the stuff," said Dickens peremptorily. His icy eyes dared Amanda to make any outcry about the child now hiccuping at his feet. With the new familiarity she hated, she was sure that he had remembered something, or heard something on the radio, to give him this dangerous concentration, and she only sent him a level look, picked up Rosie, a passive instead of a clinging weight, and started out of the hall.

Her immediate captor was behind her at once; Dickens, she realized, had wheeled purposefully into the living room. In search of the telephone? And who would answer? Almost certainly, thought Amanda, the cool-voiced woman who had made the call about the palomino mare. This night's work would have to be known only to a bare minimum of people.

A wife, or what was quaintly called a housemate? Either would belong to Dickens; the voice had the same credibility as his, and Amanda would have been willing to bet that she was as attractive as he.

Rosie quaked rhythmically against her shoulder, and this particular beleaguerment was almost more than she could bear: What if it were the onset of the kind of siege which could prostrate a longshoreman? She had read about exotic remedies like burnt feathers, but where did people get feathers?

And those relentless feet following, as though she had acquired them as permanently as her shadow. Amanda had to resist what she knew would be a disastrous impulse to whirl on the man behind her. She snapped on the bathroom light and said to Rosie, "Try to hold your

129

breath," and took a very deep breath of her own to illustrate.

Rosie, familiar with every place in the house, only gazed distractedly into the mirror over the sink. For a second, the reflection there was a terrible mockery of a family portrait: young woman holding child, man at her shoulder—with, in this brilliant examining light, something oddly smooth about his hairline. A wig.

Amanda jerked the mirror open, destroying an intolerable illusion, stared along the cabinet shelves, and took down two small plastic bottles which she placed without comment on the edge of the basin. She got an angry dark stare. "Open them."

He couldn't, at least without considerable pain. Amanda obeyed, because God knew what he might do if she said, "Open them yourself," and set them down again and walked out of the bathroom. Behind her, water began to rush fiercely into the basin as if he planned to soak his hideous red hand.

Suppose she simply kept on walking, as if in obedience to further orders? He might easily have sent her for something like Epsom salts—and she had Rosie, and in the kitchen there was the back door.

And outside the back door there was the virgin snow. It was at least three hundred yards to the nearest house, black under its grove of cottonwoods when she had passed it earlier; how far would she get before Dickens realized that it was taking her a long time to find the medication and came plunging after her?

In the kitchen, Amanda switched on the light, heartbeat accelerating as she gazed at her pink plaid eggcup soaking in the sink, an unreal reminder of the perfectly normal morning that seemed like several days ago. Was it conceivable that in his preoccupation with his hand the creature in the bathroom had left the Volkswagen

130

keys in the ignition? She couldn't remember taking them out, although there were things you did so automatically that they left no impression, and she had put her handbag down on the hall chest when she picked up Rosie.

It was worth a try, even though the thought of failure and discovery terrified her. Rosie gave a listless hiccup and Amanda moved soundlessly across the kitchen, charting the distance around the house and the obstacles in the way—and Dickens was in the hall, was rounding the corner. She pivoted and had a cabinet open when he put his head around the door, saying sharply, "Let's go."

Reaction had gotten to her hands, so that the glass she reached for rocked and sent another one toppling. "I've got to stop these hiccups first. She nearly died of them once," lied Amanda, growingly afraid of this escorted trip out into the dark. Face under control, she turned to look unwaveringly at him. "It's perfectly possible, you know."

"Oh, for Christ's sake!" said Dickens explosively, but his regard was wary as well as disgusted. The child was his lever, the carrot Amanda would follow. He consulted his watch as she filled the glass and held it to Rosie's lips—waiting for what? No one was going to drive up and rescue her, everybody in the world was asleep except her and Rosie and Dickens and Ellie Peale's murderer.

"She's got two minutes," he said.

At St. Swithin's Hospital, blond and curly-haired Mrs. Syce, having returned to the nurses' station for coffee after helping with breathing therapy for a half-drugged and protesting postoperative patient, glanced up at the bank of lights and said, "Oh, no, not again."

"Not again what?" In view of the weather and the close approach of Christmas, this wing was surprisingly quiet, and Mrs. Peralta, on duty at the desk, was trying to decipher a letter from her son in South Korea: It appeared that he wrote in the dark, with a broken goose quill.

"Six-twelve, the woman with the stroke. Someone told me she's one of our volunteers, by the way. She can't have any more sedation until three o'clock, but I can't get her quieted down."

". . . Oh. Mark says that the penalties for pot are very stiff, but in the village the bars sell a drink that's actually embalming fluid," reported Mrs. Peralta absorbedly.

"The mysterious East," said Mrs. Syce, and walked resignedly along the corridor to Mrs. Balsam's room.

Chapter 13

In her nightmare, Mrs. Balsam had been sewn tightly into a black bag which kept getting into her mouth when she tried to scream. She woke, heart thudding, to the blessed feeling of air and space around her, and then the gradual realization that half of the nightmare was reality. She was voiceless.

In spite of excellent eyesight—she wore glasses only for driving—she had always harbored a fear of going blind, but it had never occurred to her to worry about losing the faculty of speech. Now, to quiet her heart, she tried to concentrate on the more cheerful aspects of her situation, reminding herself that it might be only temporary, that she had complete faith in Dr. Simms and St. Swithin's was a very good hospital, that sixty-seven was not antique.

Such was the cling of the sleeping pill, along with her sense of deliverance from the muffling black bag, that she only rediscovered her paralyzed right side when

133

she attempted to turn to a more comfortable position, and remembered all over again what had sent her here.

The signal cord was clipped to the draw sheet where her left hand could find it automatically. Mrs. Balsam pulled it, and lay trembling in the half-dark.

Her memory was blank in spots, like a roll of defective film on which some pictures had not come out. She knew that she had gotten out of her car, although she had no recollection of where she had been going or why she had started back to the house, and that in a mirror inside she had seen the sudden impossible reflection of a man's face contorted in a grimace.

It was a dark-stubbled face alien to Mrs. Balsam's world, the kind that she imagined sprang out of hiding in the back of cars left unlocked or waited in shadowy apartment-building lobbies. Her doors were secure; she had not left the house since the morning of the day before; Apple had not uttered a single bark. So he had been concealed inside—a crawl space came to mind, because he had seemed to be rising up in the mirror—for at least that long, while she had thought herself alone.

He hadn't seen her. In shock and simple horror at all those unsuspecting hours, she had whirled and started back to her car, where Apple waited, intending to drive to the police station—and there the film went empty. She recalled a girl in a puzzling brown uniform, and then the hospital and the doctor, and finally Amanda.

Who had said she would take care of the Afghan and the mare and bring some personal belongings to the hospital, and who must be warned if it was not already too late.

Before she had been implacably sedated, Mrs. Balsam had tried to force "cellar" out of her stony throat, from a conviction that the man had been nowhere in the house proper; mightn't they attach significance to that, when she had been found outside? Now, straining again to unite brain and vocal cords (or was that a good idea? Would her treacherous body obey her only once, with no one to hear?) she produced only harsh exhalations and then, in a queer tone which she would not have recognized as her own, "shell."

Her tongue and lips were awkward and half frozen, but was it a slur or a subconscious prompting? She was of a different generation than her niece and remembered very well the commotion over bomb shelters: the single-minded pros, the moralistic cons. It seemed inexplicable that she could possess one without knowing it; on the other hand, her house was the right age, and such a place would be windowless, descended into from within. Where, in that particular area, she couldn't imagine nor did she care; her mind could grapple only with the immediate issue of warning Amanda.

It never entered her head to believe that the man had departed hours ago, any more than it would have to assume that a rattlesnake coiled beside a path was fast asleep. He was clearly not an ordinary thief, or robber or burglar or whatever the precise definition was, and if he had worn that furious grimace when he thought himself unobserved, how would he look if he were suddenly surprised by Amanda?

The propped door opened wider, the light flooded on, a nurse who looked remarkably like Harpo Marx came in. Mrs. Balsam half remembered her from earlier blood-pressure and temperature checks. She flipped off the signal light, made an automatic inspection of the I.V. needle, said cheerfully, "Would you like a drink of water? No? Warm enough?"

Mrs. Balsam gazed piercingly up at her. She had decided to try for "cellar" again, because "shelter" by itself did not mean much. She opened her mouth and instructed her throat, and nothing happened; she was as helpless as a year-old child handed a pencil and told to draw a capital B.

Her muscles felt stretched to snapping point. She tried to will her eyes full of a plea to wait, but the nurse's attention was now disapprovingly on the old-fashioned crank at the foot of the bed. "My goodness, I didn't realize that we had so many of these relics left. Tomorrow we'll get you into a bed with controls you can work yourself."

In a matter of moments, thinking that another human presence had been needed as reassurance, she would be gone. Mrs. Balsam put her lips together and uttered desperately, *"Man."*

To her own ears it sounded exactly as she had meant it to, a complete and emphatic noun. The nurse glanced down at her with surprise and congratulation. "Your niece, you mean. I remember her name because I have a Siamese called Amanda. Oh, Dr. Simms is going to be very pleased with you."

As though this small triumph were what she had been summoned to hear, she began to move toward the door, mind already elsewhere as she said automatically, "All set now?"

A new trail had been offered. Holding the round and lively eyes with her own, Mrs. Balsam got her good arm free of the covers and pointed awkwardly across herself in the direction of the telephone which, as standard hospital practice, was placed so as to be reached with ease only by healthy acrobats.

Call Amanda, she begged intensely, and the nurse, following the gesture and recognizing its urgency, said soothingly, "Yes, your niece called to ask about you, hours ago, from your house."

She studied her patient's expression. She said kindly, "If you're worried about all this snow, I wouldn't. Most likely she heard the weather reports, and stayed there. Good night now."

She was gone and Mrs. Balsam was in the semidark again, staring at the wedge of dimly lighted corridor and a situation she had never even contemplated.

She had forgotten about the snow predicted for tonight. Was it possible that Amanda, wondering about road conditions in the morning, would sleep at the house so as to be at the source of supply when she was ready to leave for the hospital? In that case, what if the man came up out of hiding again, and Apple barked and Amanda got up to see why?

Mrs. Balsam, instantly tense all through what she could feel of her body and aware that her heart was beating uncomfortably, made a conscious effort to breathe slowly and evenly. Establishing even that faulty communication with the nurse had taken its toll: Her throat muscles quivered spasmodically, her good arm felt leaden from its abortive attempt at a message, confusion was seeping into her head like mist.

After a few minutes she flexed the fingers of her left hand experimentally. She was not as deft with it as many right-handed people, thanks to a wrist broken and badly set years ago, but still . . . Knowing the reaction it would bring, even though her volunteer work had never led her into these sober precincts, she put on her bed light again.

This time there was almost no wait. The approaching tread had the crispness of beginning exasperation, and when the blonde nurse entered she snapped the signal light off like someone dispatching a persistent mosquito. "Yes?"

In spite of this menacing promptitude, Mrs. Balsam

137

had had time to decide that she would not even try for the police: What credence would they give to the tale of an elderly woman who had suffered a stroke? Besides, her one brush with officialdom had not been felicitous.

Three years ago, in the Heights, she had glanced out a window just after dark to see a flashlight bobbing intermittently around the back of the house next door. The owners were in Europe, and had asked the Balsams to keep an eye on the place now and then. With her husband away, and after some debate with herself because it was barely possible that this was some checking-up relative, Mrs. Balsam had called the police.

They had come, shone their own flashlights around, knocked at her door to report, and gazed significantly at the empty martini glass which had seemed to swell to the size of a brandy snifter; it was clear that as soon as they were outside they would say, "Another of those old dollies putting it away alone." Mrs. Balsam was vindicated by the fact that the neighbors came home three days later to find empty spaces where their two television sets, new electric typewriter, and coin collection had been, but her faith was toppled.

Now, pinning the nurse's regard with a watch-this intensity, she raised her left hand and made an awkward scribbling motion on the air. It looked more palsied than anything else, even to her, and the nurse's eyebrows drew in perplexity. Mrs. Balsam then fluttered her fingers as if she were typing, giving the impression of a lunatic wave, and when the nurse began a firm and admonishing, "Mrs. Balsam, Dr. Simms is *very* anxious that you—" her imprisoned voice escaped briefly. "Rye," it said.

But her beseeching tone was her undoing. "Of course it's all right," said the nurse at once, giving the unaffected hand a warm little shake. Infuriatingly, she tucked it under the covers and administered a further pat. "Now, Mrs. Balsam, you really must rest and let Nature help you."

Oh, my God, thought Mrs. Balsam wearily, I never know what mimes are doing and neither does she. A kind of fury at the Nature so piously invoked poured through her. The nurse, turning away from the bed, found her skirt seized with something like ferocity, and her patient, far from being calmed and reassured, raging up at her with her eyes.

When he had been in bed for half an hour, staring blankly into the dark and wondering if the effect of the magicians' punch were going to have a fairy-tale duration, such as a hundred years, Justin got up and drank a glass of milk, noticing that the snow had almost stopped. He then settled himself for sleep, but gradually, as if he had fueled it, his brain began to remark that it was very odd about Amanda.

He was mildly skeptical about thought transference, even though he knew people who swore they had received urgent messages from friends or relatives not seen for years. Even granted that Amanda had somehow sensed his unavailing pursuit of her all evening, there were strange elements to the call from Williams.

For one thing, Amanda was tactful; it was out of character for her to have had another man telephone him about shared events after weeks of silence. For another, Williams had said he had been trying to reach the Lopezes, and why would he do that? At some point his short interchange with Maria Lopez had unfurled itself before Justin like a tape, and there was something in it about waiting frantically for Amanda because of a flight east for Christmas.

No doubt there were related Lopezes, but if they were of a closeness to be informed of Rosie's whereabouts at a late hour why weren't they in charge of her in the first place?

These were niggling little points, embroidery around the central fact that after all this time Amanda had suddenly chosen to let him know in detail about Mrs. Balsam and Rosie and the horse and the dog. If he had obeyed his earlier impulse and driven to the house, he would not now be lying in the dark, a witness to the unhappy marriage of milk and beer.

Like many impulses not acted upon, this one grew in reproach. What if there had been more to that relayed report, something which Williams had deliberately omitted and could pretend to have forgotten? Not twenty feet from the rear of the duplex was the shed which housed summer maintenance equipment: wheelbarrow, gardening implements, power mower, and red five-gallon gas can. Full or empty?

Justin got up and dressed, knowing from experience that at this rate sleep was a good two hours away. Fifteen minutes later, having replenished his tank, he was on his way.

The roads would be treacherous when the snow had been traffic-melted and refrozen, but for the moment presented no difficulties apart from an occasional tendency to drift. Justin had the night to himself; even the little town center he passed through was fast asleep. He had been to Mrs. Balsam's house two or three times, but the arroyo still took him by surprise and after his unexpectedly swift descent into it he had to coax the car up the other side like a skier mounting a slope.

A half mile beyond that, another car had come to real grief, tilted sharply off the road, not near anything except a dim shape which Justin remembered to be an old church. In spite of its unfamiliar cant and cloaking of snow, it looked vaguely like Amanda's. When Justin stopped his own car, visited by surmise on this particular stretch of road, and crossed to brush the driver's window clear and beam his flashlight in, it was Amanda's.

Left here quite a while ago, by the depth of blown white, and neatly locked. Amanda had certainly walked away from it. Had the steering gone, sending her off the road? She would have had to return to Mrs. Balsam's to do any telephoning, assuming that the line was in order at that time. Had she been trying to reach him while he was ingesting that frightful mixture at the party, or driving Lucy Pettit to the restaurant?

His ego hoped so; common sense suggested that maybe Williams lived in the neighborhood, maybe Amanda had met him through her aunt. The original idea must have been for him to drive her home with Rosie, but—what? The clock unwatched over a drink, Rosie growing fretful because it was past her bedtime, Amanda deciding that it would be simpler to spend the night.

And saying, somehow incomprehensibly, "By the way, would you call Justin Howard and tell him I'm here?"

Funny that Williams hadn't mentioned the disabled car, but perhaps he considered Amanda's problems to be his affair exclusively. Justin closed his door with force and drove off to Mrs. Balsam's.

Amanda was still awake, if not actually up; two long slots of light shone in the bedroom end of the otherwise darkened house. While Justin had been concocting arguments and seizing on inconsistencies, she had been tranquilly getting ready for bed.

141

He had only been in this area at night, and it was a surprise to discover that the two sets of lightly snowed-over tire tracks visible on the road had both originated from this driveway. One would belong to the departing Williams, but the other? A friend of Mrs. Balsam's dropping by, unaware that she was away?

It would be unthinkable, after all his mental acrobatics, to depart without seeing his love. Justin walked to the front door and used the black iron knocker, remembering too late the volume of the Afghan's response. It would wake Rosie Lopez, he thought guiltily, and then: This time, *we* will lull her off to sleep.

The dog continued her man-eating threats. It was possible that a housecoated Amanda would not care to answer the door to a stranger at this hour, but surely she would not allow that clamor to go unchecked. Unless she was in the shower or tub? But even then, alone with a small child, she would investigate the source of the dog's alarm.

Justin went to the other end of the house and shouted Amanda's name twice up into the bare lilac branches outside the lighted windows. There was no reply; if anything, there was an antireply. The only awareness within belonged to the dog, Apple.

He raced around to the back, encountering a cactus without feeling it, frantic because every winter a number of people succumbed to gas from faulty heaters—but here, as though in refutation, a side window stood open. He pulled himself up on the sill so that he could see all of the room.

From its size and furnishing it was obviously Mrs. Balsam's, and it was just as obviously empty. The only signs of recent occupancy were a discarded pair of slippers and a robe tossed on the bed.

Why was this room alone lit, and where was Amanda?

142

The time for speculation was past. There was, Justin seemed to recall, a glass door opening on a patio. He ran to it, collecting a snowy rock on the way, and smashed a pane just above the lock. Although he thought he reached in with reasonable caution, he cut his wrist at once, but the door was open.

The Afghan had fled at the shattering of glass, but when he had found a light switch she put her head around a doorway—to the living room, Justin recognized—and peeked shyly at and then recognized him. This process took the form of prancing and bowing, after which she sat abruptly back on her haunches and regarded him with glowing expectancy.

Even to someone who did not live with her, she was asking for food or water. ". . . taking care of Apple and the horse," Williams had said of Amanda's mission here, but the dog at least had not been attended to.

"In a minute," Justin told her. He had not accoutred himself with a handkerchief in his hasty dressing, and he was dropping blood onto Mrs. Balsam's carpeting. He found a bathroom on the first try, pressed tissue against his wrist, moments later was gazing into the empty guest room.

The near twin bed had been remade without the motel perfection of the other, testimony to the child's interrupted sleep there. A fraying tip of dun-colored cloth showed under the edge of the bedspread. When Justin picked it up, because everything in this room was of importance to him, it was a shortish length of rag with a couple of knots in it.

He gave up on that. Ridiculously, as if Amanda were playing some coy game with him, he looked into the closet. It contained only hangers and a small suitcase which, from its tiny cotton underwear and striped shirt and miniature blue jeans, belonged to Rosie Lopez.

143

Why had Amanda left it behind, with no easy way to collect it in the morning?

Because an explanation had been taking shape in his mind in connection with the tire tracks which seemed to have been made at approximately the same time. Amanda, discovering that the telephone had become inoperative, might well have had second thoughts about staying here after Williams' departure; might have said to Mrs. Balsam's putative friend, arriving on his heels and probably known to her, "Would you do me a very great favor and drive us home?"

In which case, on a generally maddening night, Justin might have just missed her in his swing past her house with Lucy Pettit. This hypothesis did not explain the nonfeeding of Apple, now scraping beseechingly at his knee, or the abandonment of the suitcase—unless, instead of second thoughts, Amanda had had a genuine fright.

Was there really anything wrong with the telephone, or had the voice identifying itself as Williams simply not wanted Justin to call?

Try it, right away. Justin had had automatic intentions of closing Mrs. Balsam's bedroom window and switching off the light, as if her utility bills mattered at the moment; instead, he walked rapidly into the living room, Apple eager at his heels. Its serenity was underscored by the pretty little Christmas tree waking up on a bookcase and a novel open facedown beside the couch.

The telephone offered only emptiness when he lifted the receiver. The cord, cleanly severed, swung free. What had been by turns relief and wild anxiety and bafflement assumed an entirely different shape.

Apple placed an imploring paw on his knee. She looked ready to sob if not fed, and Justin mounted the

144

step that led to the kitchen, turned on the light, gazed blankly around at its bright tidiness, and located a large bag of dog food in the pantry. He filled her bowl, provided her with water, stood staring into the living room while she crunched at high speed.

Theories as to what had happened here, all untenable for one reason or another, blazed and tumbled through his head. Kidnap designs on the child? The Lopezes weren't targets for that. An intruder (leaving no signs of forced entry) expecting to find an elderly woman and coming upon Amanda instead? Simple enough to tie her up—she would know better than to resist—and ransack the place.

Had Mrs. Balsam gone away of her own volition; had she in fact gone away at all?

Gradually, Justin became aware that he was focusing on a splash of brownish-yellow on the living room wall opposite. Close up, there were flying, radiating specks. The substance wasn't quite dry when he touched it, and it smelled like mustard. On the rug at his feet was an answering little puddle with a few smeared glints of glass, as if someone had started to tidy up and then abandoned the effort.

He turned, measuring the distance from the kitchen. The quiet house, lying to him all along, must have echoed when that happened.

The police, he thought with a peculiar reluctance. They might smile over a hurled mustard jar; a cut telephone cord was something else again, and there was a small child involved. But there was one more thing to do here first, one place still unexplored, and for some reason it filled him with dread. The plant room.

Unlike the Christmas tree, the plants, deep green and pale, a few in flower, trailing and thrusting and burgeoning, did not wake at the passage of air but only

145

trembled a little in their damp earth-scented sleep. Justin, for whom houseplants died the instant they discovered where they were, had never envied this luxuriant collection; now he found it sharply unpleasant although the room was innocent enough.

No, not completely. Between the back wall and a tub of some leathery growth that looked freshly fed was an inch or two of navy leather strap.

A woman's handbag.

Chapter 14

At the sudden sound of the telephone giving an abbreviated scream before commencing its orderly pealing, Amanda's nerves jumped uncontrollably and water sloshed out of the glass she was holding to the protesting Rosie's lips. Was this call for her, or—?

"Don't answer it," ordered Dickens flatly.

"I have to." It took all her courage to start rapidly toward the doorway as if there could be no possible interference, administering automatic little thumps to Rosie, who had gotten water up her nostrils and was coughing and spluttering. "I told the hospital to call me at any hour and that I'd be waiting. They'll think it's very odd."

She knew that this was absurd—at any large institution shoulders would simply be shrugged; they had done their best—but her fast lie had produced in Dickens a greed to learn that Mrs. Balsam was safely dead. It flashed clearly across his face in the split second before he wheeled out of the kitchen, his previous prohibition turned into sharp purpose. "Make it quick," he said over his shoulder, "and watch it."

In the living room, the other man stared tensely as Amanda picked up the receiver, trying wildly to think of a signal in case this should be Justin. "Hello?"

"Miss Morley?"

"Yes." It was a woman's voice, crisp, authoritative, surely heard before at some unidentifiable point.

"This is Saint Swithin's Hospital—" Oh, God, thought Amanda in real horror, I've done it, I've killed Aunt Jane—"and although we don't usually do this I'm calling because Mrs. Balsam is agitating herself so about a message she wants you to have. She can't speak, you understand, but she managed to print a few words."

Dickens had edged so close that Amanda felt and twitched away from his body heat, but he needn't have; the nurse's voice had a carrying quality—and her little pause was obviously for sounds of gratification. "That's wonderful," said Amanda with difficulty. "What—was the message?"

Because it was impossible not to ask; Dickens had the means to force her to call back, and the essential damage was already done. He was listening tightly and—again that somehow dreadful tune-in—sending out not alarm but a rigid fury.

"Actually, for you to stay away from her house," said the nurse, and added apologetically, "I wouldn't take that *personally*, if I were you, but she certainly feels strongly about it at the moment."

The words seemed to bounce off the walls. "Tell her I understand," said Amanda, staring with fixity at her Christmas tree, "and that everything is—" in spite of herself her voice went uneven "—under control, and

148

I'll be in to see her in the morning." She could do at least that much for Mrs. Balsam, who had made such a desperate and ironic effort to protect her—or was she, in staking claim to a small piece of the future, doing it partly for herself?

She put the receiver down in the kind of silence which might explode if someone lit a match. It came to her with a rush of astonishing bitterness that where she ought to have been rejoicing at what had to be an improvement in her aunt's condition she had in fact thought, Why? Why *now*?

And Dickens had to be looked at, sooner or later. Amanda stepped away and turned her head deliberately. He had either recovered from his rage or slid into a deeper one, because although his gaze drove at her like blue sleet he showed his white teeth at her in an oblong smile. "So," he said almost pleasantly, and let his contemplation rove down to her feet. "Better put on some boots or something, you may be doing a little walking." His glance touched Rosie, who, Amanda realized with sudden dread, was raising her hand uncertainly to her mouth. "Leave her here."

Very briskly, as if the mere fact of motion could sidetrack the disastrous notion dawning in the child's head, Amanda set her down in the small armchair beside the telephone table. She could not be allowed to cry, because Dickens' new civility was not really that at all and he was now under a new pressure. Amanda started out of the room, and Rosie said piteously but with the beginnings of determination, "Where my raggie?"

It was the one thing about which she was not so much difficult as impossible. The fraying strip of cloth was guarded in the Lopez household like the family jewels, laundered by hand so that it should not join an occasional sock in some mysterious limbo created by the washing machine—and it was back at Mrs. Balsam's house.

"I'll get it for you," said Amanda.

In her bedroom, lighting a cigarette with the smoke-allergic murderer in mind, she was glad of this challenging diversion; it kept her from thinking about what was going on in the living room. Dickens didn't care how wet her feet got. He was now faced with the fact that Mrs. Balsam was alert and aware, and, provided with a detailed description of him, would take her pencil and print his name.

. . . She had a very pale pink linen scarf, but as Rosie was given to putting her talisman in her mouth the texture would be unacceptable. The satin binding on her white wool blanket was also white, but it would have to do. With her nail scissors, hands tending to shake, Amanda severed an approximating length, tied two knots in it close to one end so that it bore some resemblance to the tangled original, and crumpled it instinctively into her pocket as fast, hard footsteps crossed the front hall. When Dickens appeared in the doorway she was tying one low fur boot.

"I didn't tell you to take all night about it."

There was a near-intimacy about his sharpness, but for just a flash there had been something in his gaze so frightening that to keep herself from identifying it Amanda said the first thing that came into her head. "He's making you do this, isn't he? You don't even seem to like him very much."

In the telephone booth there had been too little space for him to hit her; here, with the bed between them, there was too much, but the same impulse was there. "Mind your own goddamned business," said Dickens in a tight snarl, and although it should have

150

had a ludicrous ring under the circumstances it did not. He jerked his head at her. "Get going."

All of Amanda's nightmares had to do with extreme heights—and this, waking, was the high diving board with no water in the pool, the dizzying lip from which there was no hope of a broken fall because the cliff curved inward. She walked stiffly ahead of Dickens into the living room, concentrating on the child in the telephone chair.

"Look, Rosie." She was bright about it, drawing the white satin ribbon from her pocket as triumphantly as if they were alone. She had to be bright, because a buried memory was beginning to stir; she could feel it growing an icy frill around her ribs. "Raggie. I washed and ironed him."

On any other occasion it would have been as impossible to deceive the child in this matter as to soothe a bereaved mother by offering an alien infant, but Rosie's need for comfort was so desperate that she hesitated for only a second before putting out a wondering hand. While Amanda held her breath, because this was of paramount importance, she fingered one of the snowy knots, her haggard little face absorbed, and put it testingly in her mouth. At an incredulous snicker from the killer she snatched it out again, flinching against the chair back.

Amanda spun, her control snapped. "You *savage.*"

The next few seconds went by so fast that she was not even sure who was responsible for what. The flat face sharpened with rage, the long eyes blazed as though matches had been lit in them, he came out of the doorway at her. Dickens, also in motion, barked a single odd-sounding syllable. An end table went crashing, carrying a lamp and an ashtray with it, Amanda's thigh met a bookcase corner with astonishing pain—and sud-

151

denly everything stopped, and she was standing there with her heart knocking coldly in her throat.

Ellie Peale had said something like that just before she died, observed the pounding blood, and there had been no one to restrain the man who was like a wolf leaping out of its cage. Dickens might be acting under duress of some kind—there was no mistaking the barely contained anger that had been emanating from him, unconnected with Amanda—but in a moment of crisis he was in command.

That he had intervened was not, she recognized, steadying herself unobtrusively against the bookcase because her legs had gone boneless with reaction, reassuring in the least; he was taking care of her as he would take care of a pack animal which was the only means to safe ground. She made herself look at him, as if by doing so she could escape from that other balked stare, and his eyes flashed steadily back at her, more icily warning than anything he could have said.

And from the corner of the chair came a series of snuffling gasps. Rosie knew the punishment for crying —one side of her face was still slightly swollen—but the explosion of violence had been too much for her.

Amanda reached her and picked her up as Dickens made a purposeful move, but he was only retrieving the toppled lamp, which was now flaring crazily down the room at the Christmas tree, and the ashtray. There had been a single cigarette end in it; he picked that up too and rubbed a sprinkle of ash into the rug with his shoe.

So that the room should look calm and orderly when—

"Okay," said Dickens, and now he did walk toward her. "Hand her over."

Amanda's arms tightened helplessly, because they were about to go out into the night again, she with the man who moments ago would have killed her with his hands, injury or not; Rosie with Dickens, who didn't like children and had a low threshhold of annoyance.

She said over the tumbled dark head cradled against her shoulder, "You'd better keep it in mind that this child is known to half the doctors and nurses in Albuquerque."

So that if you think there was a hue and cry over Ellie Peale . . .

Dickens exhibited his white and wintry teeth as he took Rosie from her, carelessly, as if she were a bundle of draperies destined for the cleaner. "You keep it in mind," he said, and snapped off the lamp.

There was clearly no need for communication between the two men; they had taken care of that while Amanda, dispatched to her bedroom, was fashioning the ribbon talisman now clutched so tensely in Rosie's fist. Amanda smiled at her, her mouth feeling as stiff as canvas, but in return got only a dubious flicker, as for a stranger whose intentions had not yet been determined. How long before the child would trust anyone again?

In the hall, Dickens paused alertly, staring at the Irish wool scarf hanging from the coatrack. "Put that over your head," he ordered.

Because they were in Amanda's territory, and top-gathered hair would make a distinctive silhouette in the unlikely event of other headlights washing through the Volkswagen? To reach the scarf she had to pass a small round mirror, recessed in pottery like a miniature well, and at once the memory which had been lying in wait reached out and struck at her.

Eyes. Not mirrored but seen across a steel examining table on which crouched her miniature black poodle—twelve years ago, thirteen? He had been hit by a car, but glancingly, and because the only evidence of dam-

153

age was a trickle of blood from one nostril, Amanda, knowing nothing of the internal injuries sustained when there was no massive bone structure as a shield, had thought he would be all right and have learned his lesson and never go near the road again. She did register the fact that the poodle, usually a dramatic trembler in these antiseptic surroundings, did not even quiver when one of his lower eyelids was pulled down.

The vet had said calmly, "Okay, William," after a long look, and injected the contents of a syringe under the passive black wool. William had subsided gently under Amanda's fingers, on his way to death although she didn't know it then.

But that look: detached, dispassionate, for a creature about whom the ultimate and necessary decision had been made. All these years later, in her bedroom doorway, a man she had never seen until tonight had turned it upon her.

Somehow or other, Amanda got the scarf knotted under her chin. She noted in a lunatic way that for all its feathery appearance it was quite scratchy. The murderer who was to companion her opened the front door, the hall light was extinguished, they went out into the bitter dark.

A few miles away, hours later than if broken promises had not been involved, the van in which Ellie Peale had been conducted to her death was being towed under police supervision from its hiding place by the river.

Chapter 15

The young Archibeque boys had no business being at the river. A first cousin of theirs had drowned in it that summer, swimming in an innocuous depth of water that masked a deep hole, and they had given solemn undertakings to stay away from the area at all seasons. They honored their undertakings as a rule because Ray Archibeque's reaction to disobedience did not take the form of reproachful lectures about mutual respect but was, instead, fast and physical.

Against this, on an afternoon of Christmas vacation, had to be balanced the fact that a friend of the boys had recently trapped a badger at the river, and that their father would be safely pinned to the dwindling supply of Christmas trees which, at this late date, he was selling at reduced prices. At three o'clock, Donald, nine, and Ruben, twelve, made a quiet exit riverwards.

With them they took their dog, Rusty, a freckle-faced, yellow-eyed animal who would have looked thoroughly at home in sled harness. The dog was delighted when he discovered the goal of the expedition; he often went by himself to chase squirrels or the half-wild cats abandoned as kittens, and on lucky days roll luxuriously on a putrescent carcass.

It was he who discovered the van. The afternoon was sharpening and the light beginning to dim when Donald and Ruben called him, having seen no badger tracks or indeed tracks of any kind. Instead of coming, Rusty bolted after a fugitive rustling in the underbrush, and could presently be heard doing some furious scratching. When the boys caught up with him, he was christening the front wheel of a vehicle in the immemorial fashion of his kind.

Donald confined himself to the comic strips in the evening paper. Ruben often read the front page, and looked at the televised local news, and there was frequent mention of a light-colored van in some connection with a crime.

This van was gray, and had certainly been well draped with brush and matted leaves in an isolated spot.

They had nothing for purposes of writing down the license number, and discussed and argued over it on the way home until it became a mishmash of letters and numbers. They found their father in a thunderously bad mood, preparing one of his difficult widower's dinners and demanding, "Okay, let's hear it, where you kids been?"

"Over at Pete's," said Donald, smooth and inventive although he was the younger.

So that was one thing to be recanted, right there, if they decided to say anything about their discovery.

Both boys were allowed to stay up late on nonschool

nights, and at ten-thirty Ruben could bear it no longer. He had no sense of civic responsibility, but one of excitement and anticipation of his name in the papers: "Ruben Archibeque, 12, of 8821 Grove Circle, led police . . ." A trapped badger was as nothing beside this.

He forced a reluctant Donald out of bed, because in some mysterious way his brother could sometimes blunt their father's temper, and padded into the living room and placed himself in front of the lighted television set. "Dad? Will you promise not to hit us if we tell you something?"

A can of beer came down in dangerous slow motion. "I have something to hit you for?"

"I don't think we should tell him. He'll hit us anyway," said the practiced Donald.

Archibeque glared at him, drank, and squeezed the empty can into aluminum pleats. "I knew you kids had been up to something. So? I'm waiting."

He looked capable of vaulting out of his chair, in spite of his exaggeratedly patient posture, and Ruben hastily offered the evening newspaper, folded to a story on the lower left side of the front page. "We went looking for the van at the river and I bet anything we found it," he said, and then, to further bury the three dangerous words, "It's this kind of light gray and it's locked and it was all covered up with branches and stuff and it has a New Mexico license plate."

The tale of actually searching for the van, like boy detectives, was so preposterous that it succeeded. Archibeque, who had started galvanically at the mention of the river, sank back in his chair, his dumbfounded gaze swiveling slowly from Ruben to Donald, who, briefed at the last minute, was wearing an expression of pride and virtue.

157

Long, chancy seconds went by before Archibeque glánced down at the paper, glanced up again, asked, "Whereabouts at the river?"

. . . Wallet with driver's license, the required glasses, gold cigarette lighter which had been the last anniversary present from her husband: proof, as if it had been required, that Mrs. Balsam had not planned a departure. But her Rabbit was gone—with whom at the wheel, and what vehicle accompanying or following it?

Justin abandoned thought. For lack of anything better to do with it, he thrust the handbag back into hiding and took the time to stuff towels into the glassless space in the patio door before he switched off the lights and let himself out. Apple had had notions of going with him, and her sorrowful cries carried a little way into the dark.

The two sets of tracks led to the town center, but there he lost them in a sudden welter as though a party had broken up somewhere. A left turn at the first traffic light would lead him ultimately to Amanda's house; Justin persevered instead to the darkened volunteer fire station. At the back, as he had hoped, was the small police station, its lights swallowed up by drawn Venetian blinds.

The dispatcher on duty—even in his distraction it struck Justin that he looked like a heavily moustached Mona Lisa—put aside a thick volume on real-estate practice and listened attentively, although his gaze had lingered over the deep fresh scratch on Justin's wrist. At the mention of Mrs. Balsam he frowned, held up a staying finger, and pulled open a drawer. "There was something on her in the day report."

Justin lit a cigarette, his hand surprising him with a slight unsteadiness. The dispatcher scanned the sheet

158

in front of him, shook his head in silent disgust at something, flipped it over. "Here we are. At one-nineteen, patrol car two responded . . ." He trailed off, evidently feeling that the official entry was not for Justin's ears, read briefly, and glanced up. "Mrs. Balsam was found unconscious outside her house and taken by ambulance to the hospital," he said. "It looked like a stroke to the attendant."

Justin listened to the few details in blank astonishment. A natural disaster had never occurred to him in connection with Amanda's lighthearted, energetic aunt, although now that he thought about it he remembered Amanda, not a nagger, raising her eyebrows occasionally over Mrs. Balsam's brisk plying of the salt shaker at lunch or dinner. Hypertension?

Plus the discovery that she had unwarily left a door unlocked and become the victim of malicious mischief? The smashed mustard jar would be in keeping, if a semiliquid substance would have stayed dampish that long, and so might the severing of the telephone cord. Justin had not opened any drawers; for all he knew, they might have disclosed all kinds of unpleasantness.

But this theory did not explain the concealment of Mrs. Balsam's handbag, unless the parcel-delivery service girl who had found her had put it there for safekeeping, and car theft did not come under the head of mischief. Much more urgently, where was Amanda?

The dispatcher, watching with his Mona Lisa eyes, pushed the telephone across. "Maybe she's home right now," he suggested.

Justin dialed with a sense of futility. Still, he gave Amanda time to wake out of a deep sleep, peer at the clock, and walk from her bedroom to the living room at a snail's pace before he hung up.

A call came in. The dispatcher swung his chair

159

around, did some alert jotting, and then pressed keys and spoke into a transmitter, relaying an address and a string of numbers. When he turned back to Justin he was tolerant but brisk.

Women of all ages were eccentric, his shrug and spread hands implied, and young women changed their minds with frequency. What more likely than that Miss Morley had borrowed her aunt's car with her own out of commission? He did not actually say that Amanda had decided to rejoin her male companion of earlier that evening, but the possibility was clearly on the air. So was his desire to get back to his real-estate book.

Justin contained himself. He said that he had every reason to believe that his fiancée (he had boldly identified Amanda as such in order to obtain a hearing at all) had done no such thing, and that under all the circumstances he was extremely worried about her. Would the dispatcher at least put out a description of the car along with a request that Amanda call him at once?

Small-town police forces did this kind of thing routinely, and after all Mrs. Balsam was a resident. The dispatcher made a few good-tempered notes. Justin did not know the Volkswagen's plate number, so with a queer wrench at his heart he added what her driver's license said of Amanda but did not really describe her at all: five-feet-six, brown hair, hazel eyes. The child in question was about two.

"May I—" an urgent notion had entered his head "—use the phone again? It's just possible that my fiancée is at the hospital."

He didn't believe it, he didn't believe any of the suggestions offered to him, particularly that of Amanda haring off after Williams with little Rosie Lopez in tow, but here he might happen upon a trace of her and gain some enlightenment about Mrs. Balsam at the same time.

"Help yourself," said the dispatcher, furtively sliding his book closer. "Might be quickest to call Ace Ambulance and find out where they took her."

It turned out to have been St. Swithin's. By firmly establishing himself once more as Amanda's fiancé, Justin learned that Mrs. Balsam's condition was somewhat improved although still guarded; she had, in fact, been able to send a communication to her niece, to whom the nurse at the other end of the line had spoken.

"When?" asked Justin, stunned and staring at the man across the desk.

"Oh, I'd say about fifteen or twenty minutes ago."

"At her house?" Idiotic; where else could they have reached her?

"I would assume so. It's the number she left with us, anyway."

"Did Mrs. Balsam say—" began Justin, and was interrupted with a certain crispness: "I'm afraid you'd have to ask Miss Morley about that."

Justin thanked the nurse and hung up. Unnecessarily, because her voice had quacked clearly around the small office, he said, "She's home. They just talked to her."

The dispatcher tore his sheet of notes from the desk pad, crumpled it, and dropped it into a wastebasket. "All's well that ends well," he said cheerfully, and had his book open before Justin reached the door.

That simple? The invasion of the house taking place long before Amanda got there, the innocent-looking telephone going unnoticed until much later? No. It was a measure of his state of mind that Justin remembered only now the unanswered ringing on Mrs. Balsam's line all evening.

161

Amanda herself—inexplicably not answering her own telephone a few minutes ago, or had she silenced it after a long day containing a severe shock?—would explain it to him in a further few minutes. Still, he felt as tense as before, and it took a sudden sharp skid at the traffic light to ease his foot on the gas pedal. He drove the rest of the way with heightened awareness, because these were exactly the circumstances in which a heifer or other large animal would come blundering into his path.

Were the fresh furry-edged tire tracks ahead of him the ones that had left Mrs. Balsam's house? The local population was not limited to Amanda and Williams, however much it might feel that way—but the tracks separated at Amanda's empty circular driveway. One vehicle had entered at the far end. There was not a single light showing.

Amanda here, just long enough to talk to the nurse at Saint Swithin's, and gone again.

A conflagration of rage and something else sprang up in Justin's abused stomach. He reminded himself, slamming his door so hard that the car rocked, of the serene occupancy suggested by those two gold windows at Mrs. Balsam's house. False, so that perhaps this black and sleeping shape . . .

He had left his headlights on, and this time, on his way to the spare key which Amanda kept in the trough of a birdfeeder hanging outside the living room window, he made a fast examination of the footprints in the snow. One isolated set belonged to a man; the other scuffled trail, as if made by two people in single file, showed the occasional sharp indentation of a woman's high heels where they had not been dragged over.

Amanda, almost certainly Williams, and another man.

162

Justin located the key, wiped it free of snow and birdseed, and fitted it into the lock. The click of metal almost blotted out a sound from within that turned him cold: a kind of broken gasping, not quite crying. He opened the door, knew where to find the hall light switch, and stood staring down at Rosie Lopez.

Chapter 16

Claude. Late, and as if it could help her, Amanda's brain had identified the single sharp syllable with which Dickens had stopped that deadly rush in her living room. Necessity had jarred it out of him and the response had been instant, so it was the killer's real name.

She wished her brain had let it alone. Anyone might claim that he had returned from an absence to find his van stolen, but how many Claudes could be found in the immediate vicinity of any given crime? And the natural conclusion to that—

Amanda would have thought it impossible for fear to actually stop her ears, but in that herded walk to the car she caught only the echo of a wail from Rosie and then Dickens' voice, savage: "Okay, *okay,* I'll get the damned thing."

The rag, she thought; the essential talisman. With it, able to pretend that it was the real link to her parents

165

and home and safety, Rosie might fall exhaustedly asleep, not rasping dangerously at Dickens' nerves. Light from the hall flooded briefly out onto the snow as Amanda half-turned, and there in the doorway was the child in that hard and careless grip, the length of white satin dangling from her fist.

"Here." Claude thrust the Volkswagen keys at her so roughly that they seemed momentarily like something else and she stepped instinctively back, off-balance, sliding in the snow. "In," he said, "fast, and then I'll tell you where to go."

Amanda slid in behind the wheel, the corner of her eye observing the rapid dark shape of Dickens depositing his burden in the pickup. He had entered the driveway from the far end, so that once more she was presented with the plateless front of the truck. Before the discovery of the body in the church she would have found that reassuring; now it seemed only automatic deviousness, as much a part of Dickens as his clear eyes or disarming smile.

His headlights sprang on, an implacable dazzle: She would have to back out. She turned the key in the ignition, knowing that this was the last leg of the journey, the last—

Abruptly, without warning, her body became one long tremble, the gearshift and floor pedals felt as strange and terrifying as the controls of a jumbo jet. She had trouble with her breathing. She turned her head away from the merciless flare of light and said with effort, "I don't—think I can drive."

"You'll drive if you want to see that kid again." The foggy voice wasn't any more threatening than a surgeon's might have been, announcing an inoperable cancer. "Up to the corner and then left."

Amanda pulled air into the very bottom of her lungs,

let it out slowly, got the car started and backed. Her hot rush of hatred had a steadying effect, and she registered the fact that one or both of these men knew the valley, although she had never seen either of them before, so that there was no chance of saying that a road was torn up and picking an alternate route of her own.

To where, and what good would it do anyway?

She shut that reflection off, realizing it to be as dangerous as lying down to rest in a blizzard. Beside her, Claude spoke only to give last-second, monosyllabic directions: "Go straight." "Bear right." Behind her, his headlights like the hugely magnified eyes of some deadly insect, cruised Dickens.

They were proceeding roughly south, keeping away from the main roads on which, even at this hour and in this weather, there would be a certain amount of traffic. Would they risk the bus terminal, with its departures for all points? Amanda slid a glance across, and thought that at least a part of the killer's pain must have been psychosomatic; his right hand, instead of being held rigidly away from him, now rested on his knee.

He would be able to put it in his pocket. Denims were common enough, and his coatlessness on a cold and snowy night could be explained by the overheating of most terminal buildings; he might have checked it, or left it with a companion. The neatly blocked dark blond wig was transforming. How likely was it in any case, more than forty-eight hours after Ellie Peale had been forced into a van, that the police would be monitoring points of exit?

It all added up to a reasonably safe escape for Claude and also for Dickens, who could pick his moment to deposit Rosie on a bench and vanish, *if* there were no witness. Then Amanda must not get near the terminal, she—

The night was suddenly alive with a two-noted warble, rising into a more imperative siren. In the icy and echo-carrying air it was impossible to tell its direction. Claude twisted in his seat and said, "Get into that driveway, fast. Lights off."

Dickens had fallen back at once. Amanda obeyed, turning in between bordering poplars, heart thumping in a mixture of terror and hope. A second emergency vehicle burst into sound and then both died, blocks away to the east and north: an accident, frequent in this area even when the roads were clear. Claude relaxed out of his tensity. "Move. Blink your lights."

The house to which the driveway belonged slept tranquilly. Amanda backed and turned, forcing away another wave of trembling, and signaled with the headlight knob. Dickens had found a driveway of his own, and in moments the pickup was sending its warning stings after her.

How far now? Or rather, how long?

"Left," said Claude as they approached a wide four-way stop, and then, when Amanda was in the middle of the intersection, "No, *right!*"

She turned the wheel, but not fast enough for him. He seized it, and instinct sent Amanda's foot to the brake. The snow was not innocuous here; ice had formed in traffic-melted spots and the car went spinning, carrying the night with it. A stretch of adobe wall reeled by and the snow-sculpted bark of an immense cottonwood trunk loomed through the windshield before she got the Rabbit to a halt.

Incredibly, Claude swore at her. Amanda did not bother to reply that the skid had been his fault. Chest still thudding, she glanced into the rearview mirror to await Dickens' reaction to this apparent rebellion.

They were alone. In a matter of seconds, the pickup with Rosie in it had vanished.

The light gray 1972 Chevrolet van now reposing in the police garage was registered to Claude Eggen, 281a Sevilla, in the northwest quadrant. It said nothing to the naked eye, and an exhaustive examination would wait until morning. What did not wait was a warrant entitling the police to knock at Eggen's door in the small hours and search the premises if this should be indicated.

In view of the nature of the crime and the extensive publicity, plus an editorial in that evening's newspaper taking the authorities to task for the initial delay, the warrant wasn't difficult to obtain. The state police had assisted the sheriff's department from the second day on, and a unit went along as backup.

In summer, Sevilla Road was green with fields of grapes and patches of chili, its small houses deep in cottonwood shade. Less lovely sights obtruded from the snow: tractors that looked as if they had never run, a broken and dangling swing, a shack which seemed composed of tar paper and aluminum foil. Detective Carroll, in charge tonight, had made inquiries here the year before in connection with the vandalizing of a local school and remembered the atmosphere as tightly buttoned-up: These were hard-working people, it said, who kept out of trouble by minding their own business.

Two hundred-eighty-one was a cut above the rest, recently painted white cement block with, as their headlights showed, unfortunate pink scrollwork around the door. The mailbox said Patterson. The next mailbox, at the head of a long narrow driveway, said 281a and nothing else.

169

The very small house at the end of it, evidently a rental unit, was as totally dark as its neighbors. The driveway continued around one end to what was, in the headlight dazzle, a backyard containing a number of vehicles. The deputy with Carroll got out and walked to the rear of the house; Carroll approached the front door and knocked, even though the unflawed snow was suggestive.

Deputy Garcia came back, swinging his heavy flashlight. "He's got four heaps and a kind of garage setup back there," he reported. "Looks like he fixes them up and sells them."

Which might explain a bothersome point: Unlike most people, Eggen was not identified exclusively with a single vehicle.

A brief conference with the state police officer followed. They had the warrant and the back door was a flimsy one; equally, the law was full of loopholes and Garcia volunteered that he knew a woman named Claude, in which case . . . The numbering would seem to indicate that the Pattersons were the landlords of 281a, and Carroll and the deputy presented themselves under the ornamental pink scrollwork of the house next door.

Mrs. Patterson, announcing her unhurried arrival by a series of switched-on lamps, proved to be a widow in her trim and well-preserved fifties. She had the fawn-gold hair widely adopted by women of her age, and either slept in her makeup or had taken time to apply it.

She was indeed the landlady of 281a. Informed of the warrant, she widened her round brown eyes and said, "Oh, but that's ridiculous. For one thing, Mr. Eggen's been in Denver for the past couple of days, his sister's very ill there. He had a friend call me to lock up the house because he left in a terrible hurry."

"Did you know the friend?" inquired Carroll.

"No, and I didn't ask. Why should I?" demanded Mrs. Patterson, tweaking a fawn-gold curl into place and looking flinty at the same time. "It's my property, it's to my interest to protect it. Furthermore, if you'd ever met Cl— Mr. Eggen, you'd know how absurd this all is. He's a very quiet young man, and *very* polite."

Unlike present company. Something going on there, wondered Carroll? It seemed unlikely, in view of their ages and the police artist's sketch, but it needed only a quick dip into famous-crime annals to document how many women, often pretty ones, attached themselves as cheerfully as lemmings to men of dubious if not downright sinister appearance.

This woman had undoubtedly read the newspapers and looked at television—barring infants and the blind, no one in the city could have been entirely immune— and had any faint wonder or uneasiness wiped out by the ailing sister in Denver. People tended largely to believe what they wanted to, particularly if there was a personal relationship involved.

"Let's have a look at his place," said Carroll.

"Of course, I don't really know him all that well," said Mrs. Patterson, walking down the driveway with the three men. She had fallen into step with the state policeman, and her quilted robe under a coat swished around the high-heeled boots for which she had exchanged her slippers. "I'm away all day, I'm a realtor, and weekends are especially busy."

Her defensiveness was now cautiously for herself, Carroll noted, and she began to slip into the past tense. "He was quiet, as I said, and paid his rent on time, and I mean what more can you ask? He wasn't one of those

171

men with a steady procession of lady friends coming and going—"

That and its implication lay eloquently on the night air as they reached the house and Carroll used the key she had given him and opened Claude Eggen's front door. In spite of five years on the Chicago police force before coming to New Mexico, he had never lost his nape-prickling curiosity upon entering the private domain of a suspected killer. The beam of Garcia's flashlight centered on a light switch, and he snapped it on.

Some places gave themselves away by their very contradiction: Carroll remembered the appalling state of the apartment belonging to an antiseptic woman school principal, and the tenderly cared-for collection of tiny glass and china animals owned by an unemployed cab driver who had wrecked his ex-wife's house with an axe. At first glance, and in contrast, Eggen's dwelling said nothing at all.

The ten-by-twelve living room (Mrs. Patterson informed them with unjustified pride that she rented the place furnished) contained a blue couch and two small armchairs, one blue, one brown; a television set on a stand; and a magazine rack holding several copies of an automotive publication. A single small table was bare of anything except a lamp, its shade retaining dusty cellophane pleats.

The kitchen opening off to the left was tidy except for a frying pan with congealed grease on the stove and, in the sink, a dried and crusted dinner plate, knife, and fork. On the counter beside it, obvious breakfast utensils reposed in a rubber drainer. In this sector of his life, Eggen was nothing if not neat.

Garcia, the state policeman, and Mrs. Patterson had proceeded into the bedroom and Carroll joined them there, bothered by this strange featurelessness. They

172

had been assuming all along that the abduction of Ellie Peale was the result of a growing obsession which had finally slipped its leash, a spur-of-the-moment action without heed to consequences—but, consciously or otherwise, the man who lived here appeared to have erased his personality.

The bedroom was papered in a close pattern of gray and white diamonds. The brown-blanketed bed against one wall was made, the table beside it held a cheap clock-radio. (Eggen was clearly not a smoker, there wasn't an ashtray in sight.) The rest of the space was largely taken up by a bureau and a chest of drawers. Astonishingly, there was a framed photograph on the bureau.

It was in color. An attractive, blue-eyed woman whose hair and makeup and dress were an echo of twenty years ago smiled proudly into the camera, her arm through that of a handsome clear-featured boy in graduation cap and gown. Unless the girl witness, Beryl Green, suffered from myopia, the boy could not possibly be Eggen. But the small overalled child in the foreground, gazing up with a blunted profile?

Garcia had opened the closet door with a practiced thumb and forefinger on the shank of the knob, although it seemed certain that Ellie Peale had never been here. Eggan did not possess an extensive wardrobe: One hanger was occupied by a gray sports coat and slacks, a second by a heavy plaid wool shirt, a third by a raincoat in need of cleaning.

Behind Carroll, standing in the middle of the room with a landlady's all-seeing eye, Eggen's erstwhile champion said crossly, "I had this room papered just before he came in, and he's gone and smeared it."

But the very small cloud on the gray-and-white wallpaper over the bed, at the height and arm-reach of a supine man, wasn't a smudge. Up close, it was penciling, and it sent a chill through the seasoned Carroll. The state police car carried a camera and it would have to be used, the print time-dated and witnessed, to record this embryo horror until the wallpaper itself could be lifted off.

The tiny writing was arranged like a problem in addition, and Eggen had commenced with the simple, besotted equation of third-graders and then gone on to anagrams of two names:

EP-CE

Pal

Gal

Plague (This when his date invitation had been turned down?)

Leap

Chapter 17

"Hello, Rosie," said Justin to the tear-tracked little face with terror dying out of it. "Remember me? Amanda's friend."

Rosie bobbed her head fractionally. Her eyelids looked alarmingly swollen.

Justin crouched down beside her, slowly, so as to give no possible cause for new fright. "Amanda isn't here, is she?"

The bob became a decisive wag. "All gone," said Rosie out of a hoarse throat, and although Justin had heard her apply this locution to lost toys or people departed on shopping errands it had a very final sound in combination with her tears. And the prints of high heels in the snow only went one way.

I don't believe it, said Justin harshly to himself, but he picked up the child, unresisting, a strange piece of satin ribbon dangling from her fist, and looked first into the living room—empty, quiet, with a Christmas tree shin-

175

ing at him—and then went through the rest of the house, turning on lights with dread. Relief swarmed through him at the discovery of Amanda's wet calf pumps in her bedroom: She had changed into flat heels. The manicure scissors on the bed had obviously been used to carve out the object which Rosie clutched.

A washcloth was called for—the child's face was a glistening embodiment of distress—but it would have to wait. Justin headed for the living room and the telephone, getting confirmation from Rosie on the way that there had been two men with Amanda. Had they hurt Amanda? He got a doubtful no.

The enigmatic-eyed dispatcher already had all the background information, but events in this area would fall under a different jurisdiction. Justin called the sheriff's department and went through the whole business again. Because of the lack of any sign of violence in the house the voice at the other end was inclined to be skeptical. Amanda was well over eighteen, and missing people were generally missing of their own volition although family and friends were reluctant to accept it.

"Look," said Justin, his own voice hardening, "I know this girl, and she would never under any circumstances leave a child of two alone in a pitch-black house. To hell with this, give me the sheriff's home number and I'll call him and after that I'll call—"

He was told hastily to calm down. He repeated the description of the car registered to Jane Balsam, and added that if they had thoughts of sending anybody to the house he wouldn't be there; he was going to try following the tire tracks himself, taking Rosie Lopez with him.

This led to strong official demurs. They didn't know Justin, surely he would understand that, and in the absence of the parents or an official guardian the child should be placed under the care—

"Take me to court," said Justin, and clapped the receiver down. His car would scarcely have had time to get cold, but he went rapidly back to Amanda's bedroom for a blanket to wrap Rosie in, taking the pillow as well: Bundled up on the back seat, she might sleep.

A harried compassion made him spend fifteen seconds with washcloth and towel. Then, with a feeling of surrealism—Lucy Pettit's apartment, Mrs. Balsam's house, and now Amanda's—he switched off the lights and carried Rosie out to his car. "Raggie," she said surprisingly to him, exhibiting her peculiar trophy as he improvised her bed, and Justin, finally recognizing this as a companion piece to the knotted cloth in Mrs. Balsam's guest room, said, "Raggie. Right."

The tire tracks bore south, angling at times to keep away from a main road to the east. An occasional horse moved in a snowy field, the only break in the sleeping stillness. Justin shut his mind to everything but the earlier progress in his headlights, puzzled over a split-up into driveways fifty yards apart with no footprints in either place, continued following.

And arrived at a wide four-way stop, with some wild skidding evident. One vehicle had turned west, the other east. Which had carried Amanda?

"Where did he go, where has he taken that child?" asked Amanda fiercely. She had to school her voice so that it wouldn't shake. To have been goaded about like an animal for all these hours and then lose Rosie completely—

"Making arrangements," said Claude briefly. Gone at once, but blazing through Amanda's brain like a rocket, was a sly and secretive tuck of the mouth corner she could see in the light from the dashboard. "We call him

in ten minutes and he'll tell you where to pick her up."
He consulted his watch, somehow elaborately. "Get
going."

A night of instructions like repeated rasps; skin so
subjected might begin gently to bleed. But for just a
moment Claude had been entertained—at what?
Scarcely his own situation, so it had to be hers.

Amanda put the car into gear, straining over this new
element. He had mocked at Rosie's rag, but that association had to be long gone. *The rag,* gripped with all the
strength of which Rosie was capable when Amanda had
been forced to give her to Dickens. Was it really likely
that she would have dropped it, her sole comforter, in
the course of the few steps to the front door?

Outside, Dickens had said loudly and furiously that
he would "get it" upon Rosie's wail—but she would
have cried out if she were pinched suddenly, creating
an excuse for the reopening of the door. Amanda had
seen her clearly framed there, but what about the seconds when her attention had been distracted by
Claude?

"Take a right," he said beside her.

Amanda swung the wheel automatically, looking at
the unmarked white road before her, coming up to
something else in her own mind. Why, at this point,
would Dickens have continued to burden himself with
a child for whom he had only strong dislike and con-
tempt when there was an obvious place to leave her?
On the other hand, he had been carrying something
when he walked so speedily around his truck, and in
that short space of time there wasn't—

Yes, there was. Amanda's lined raincoat, hanging
ready to his hand in the hall. Lightly crushed, carried
just so, it would have passed in the dark for a human
weight. Minutes ago at the intersection Claude had dis-

tracted her a second time, so that, the pickup vanished into the night, she should think herself in even deeper thrall.

And thus lose sight of the fact that she was driving to her death, that she was alive only because a suitable site had not yet been reached.

It was one thing to have recognized the seal set upon her by Dickens in her bedroom doorway; it was another now that the abstract was becoming real. Again Amanda's lungs did not seem to be getting enough air, and it was with difficulty that she managed what would have been the normal thing to say if she were still deceived: "Isn't it about time to find a telephone booth?"

If she had had any smallest doubt about her reconstruction of events it would have been dissipated by Claude's extreme glibness. "There's one up ahead, about a mile."

A spasm of actual nausea quivered through Amanda's stomach. She did not travel this road often, but she remembered a picnic area with benches and trestle tables under trees but no toilet facilities, so that it might be weeks or even months before—

Slow the car enough to jump out and commence a blind and hopeless run in the snow? Try to engineer an accident which would involve only the passenger side of the car? A racing driver might have attempted it; Amanda knew that she could not. Even in this extremity her sense of survival was too strong for inexpert aiming at a tree or a telephone pole.

Far ahead, well past the picnic area in this crystal air —in fact at a main junction—were tiny, shifting Christmas lights. No, not Christmas lights, but pinpoints of red being blanked out occasionally as if by intervening figures. "You'd better open your window," said

Amanda with an air of defiance, staking everything on a diversionary tactic of her own, "because I'm going to smoke a cigarette. Incidentally, there's somebody behind us."

Claude twisted as she reached for the cigarettes and matches on the dashboard. Her foot went down on the accelerator, not in a sudden burst of speed which might cause a skid but in a steadily building pressure, and he turned back at once, saw the distant roadblock, and ripped a few savage words at her as he snatched the keys out of the ignition.

The car continued to travel, weaving and slewing as Claude lunged across Amanda and reached the headlight control, sending them into darkness. He kicked at her ankle and found the brake. For a matter of seconds he was engaged with the wheel, jerking the hood away from a fence of railroad ties black against the snow, and Amanda's trembling hands found the folder of matches deposited in her lap, struck one and held it to the others, thrust it wildly at the face now as close to hers as it had been to Ellie Peale's.

She got the door open in the middle of his shriek of rage and pain, and with the car still rolling wrenched herself free of his weight and the floor pedals and went pitching out and down to the road. Even with the snow as cushion the impact dizzied her. She staggered upright and began to run, hearing behind her the slam of the Rabbit's door.

And here came Dickens, bearing down on her with the cruel white-gold flare of high beams. He was shouting at her. Her whole life experience shriveled to the scope of hours, the tears she had not allowed earlier pouring down her face, Amanda reached the guard rail on the bridge that crossed an irrigation ditch, swung herself terrifiedly over it, and dropped.

She had never looked consciously at the ditch when she drove over it—it was simply there, like the mountains and the far cottonwoods—and it was deeper than she would have guessed. Her ankle gave and she went plummeting down one steep side on her back, her head arrested by sudden agonizing contact with a rock or an iron tree root. Above her, as if in fury gone mad, a horn was blaring.

And she had been wrong, and ruined everything, because when the nightmarish noise had stopped, clods of snowy dirt were disturbed on the ditch bank and a triumphant voice reduced to a mutter by the rush of blood in her ears was saying, "I've got her. I've got Rosie. . . . *Amanda.* Are you all right?"

It was Justin she had fled from moments ago, Justin who was now sliding a cautious arm under her shoulders and attempting to lift her to a sitting position. Amanda lifted her bursting, throbbing head cooperatively, and, to the accompaniment of a chopped-off siren and what turned out later to have been a warning shot from the police, went for a short time completely to pieces.

Somewhere in this process there was a shattering collision of metal, followed by shouts. "There goes my car," observed Justin.

He was correct. At the sight of Amanda's running, stumbling figure with the Rabbit beyond, he had swung his car broadside, plucked Rosie from the back seat, leaned in to send that signaling echo of horn to the roadblock ahead while his bright lights beaconed into the night. Claude Eggen, slewing the Rabbit around and hearing a siren come to life, had rammed the obstructing car. He had been apprehended with his wig badly singed and melted.

Tow trucks were sent for. A deputy drove Justin and Amanda to the house which she had left with Dickens' pronouncement upon her. En route, he phoned in the location of the church in which Ellie Peale's body reposed, and then a description of the man whom Mrs. Balsam would identify, still by means of printing, as a shaven Harvey Sweet.

Before Amanda gave the statement which would have to be elaborated in detail, before she drank the coffee Justin made and laced heavily with rum—mystifyingly, he was at the same time supplying himself with Port du Salut which he tucked anyhow into rolls—she put Rosie to bed in her tiny guest room. She said, leaving the door propped wide so that the child could not wake to darkness but only a golden twilight, "They're all gone, Rosie, they really are."

And presently, to Justin in the living room, "I know he won't come back, but will you stay?"

Justin simply looked at her.

Late in the morning, Amanda learned that a button corresponding to the others on Ellie Peale's bloodied shirt had been disinterred from one of the split seats in Claude Eggen's van. Astonishingly, he and the man she could never think of as anything but Peter Dickens were half brothers. Had the mere fact of looks been a leverage, growing over the years?

She put that firmly out of her mind, and went with Justin to see her aunt, bringing nightgowns and bed jackets, books and cologne, flowers and liqueur-centered cherries. Mrs. Balsam's brilliant eyes, no longer burning with messages but absorbed with the process of recovery, went from one face to the other. She still could not manage many sounds, but she said what was unmistakably intended to be, "Good."

The team of men going meticulously through her house had discovered the trap door to the bomb shelter under the apparently unflawed carpeting in the area described to them. Amanda had firmly declined an invitation to go down the ladder; illogical although she knew it to be, it seemed to her that little wisps of horror might still linger there.

"Shelter?" she said later to Justin, who was scrupulously measuring for glass to be replaced in the patio door. *"Shelter?"*

Justin studied her, let his steel tape whistle back into place, and clipped on the Afghan's leash—not easy, because with friends restored she was a silky and importunate bustle. He was aware of the dark breath of last night touching Amanda. He said conversationally, "Do you realize that without even being married yet we have acquired a child and a dog?"

Rosie, still hollow-eyed but engrossed in a banana of which Apple wanted a piece, swiveled her great gaze briefly back and forth.

"Working models only," said Amanda.